Shadow Shark

Other books by Colin Thiele

Shadow Shark

Colin Thiele

Harper & Row, Publishers

Library of Congress Cataloging-in-Publication Data
Thiele, Colin.
  Shadow shark.

  Summary: Two cousins join a group of fishermen in
pursuit of a massive shark off the coast of Southern
Australia.
  [1. Sharks—Fiction.   2. Sea stories.   3. Australia—
Fiction]   I. Title.
PZ7.T354Si 1988   [Fic]   87-45566
ISBN 0-06-026178-1
ISBN 0-06-026179-X (lib. bdg.)

Shadow Shark

1

Joe was playing with Mophead. They were in the middle of the main street. There was no traffic. A tiny town like Cockle Bay rarely saw more than three or four cars in an hour.

Joe threw the ball as hard as he could, and Mophead went pounding after it. His paws skidded on the gravel and sent up little clouds of dust as he overtook the ball and snapped it up in his mouth. Then he trotted back to Joe with a big look of triumph on his face.

Mophead belonged to nobody and everybody. He was a stray. But instead of being shot at in the sheep paddocks by angry farmers, or run over by fishermen driving loaded trucks of tuna, he had somehow survived and become famous. He had adopted the town, and in the end the town had adopted him. People even called him the Town Dog. They liked to see his happy clumsy body standing patiently outside the butcher's shop waiting for a handout, or hurtling dangerously down the street after his sloppy half-chewed tennis ball, or lying under the shady pepper trees on hot summer days. But in spite of that, nobody wanted him as a pet. Nobody wanted him at home.

Joe and Mophead had a lot in common. In one way they were both strays. Joe's father was dead and his mother had gone away, so now he was living with Uncle Harry and Aunt Ellen and his two cousins, Meg and Maureen.

Cockle Bay was a big change after Melbourne. It was a tiny place on the coast of South Australia where the land curved up around the Great Bight, the huge arc of water separating Australia from the Antarctic Ocean. Once it had been a busy little port, with regular sales of cattle and sheep and a crane on the jetty loading wheat and wool into the coastal ketches. But all that was gone. Now the town rarely saw anyone except a few local fishermen and farmers and a handful of vacationers looking for a peaceful spot as far away as possible from the city.

Joe threw the ball again, and Mophead raced off after it like a rocket. It curved over toward the sidewalk in front of the Commercial Hotel and started to slow down, bouncing along a few inches above the ground. But Mophead didn't slow down. His head was low, his eyes were fixed on nothing but the ball. The ball and the dog reached the corner of the hotel together. Mophead's jaws were thrust forward and his mouth was just opening ready to snap it up.

Crash!

Old Porker Bacon, the handyman at the hotel, had chosen that particular moment to come around the corner on his bike. He was wobbling even more than usual, trying to adjust a bagful of bottles between the handlebars. Mophead hit the front wheel—head-on. His big shoulders knocked it out from under Porker Bacon and sent the whole bike skidding along the sidewalk on its side. A terrible sound of breaking glass came from the bag. Porker landed on his back with a thud and lay there for a while, stunned. Mophead gave a little yelp and stopped for a second. But he still had his eye on his goal. Leaping aside from Porker and his spread-eagled bike, he lunged at the ball and snapped it up.

"Oh my gosh," Joe cried, and ran forward. It wasn't the first time he had seen Mophead scatter someone over the sidewalk. He arrived, panting, just as Porker sat up. "Are . . . are you all right, Mr. Bacon?"

Porker put his hand up to his head and felt it gingerly. A lump was beginning to grow above his left ear.

"That rotten, flea-bitten mutt," he said. "He'll kill someone before long." He looked at Mophead balefully. "If somebody doesn't kill him first."

"Gee, I'm sorry," Joe said. "I didn't expect you to come around the corner like that."

"Yeah, yeah, yeah," Porker growled, still feeling his head. "I've told you before—go and play out in the paddock, not here in the main street."

Mophead put the ball down on the ground between Porker and Joe. It was a sloppy mess, slimy with saliva. Porker wrinkled his nose in disgust at the sight of it. "Uggh." Mophead wagged his tail and looked at Joe and Porker expectantly.

"He wants to play with you," Joe said.

"I'll play with him all right," Porker answered. "I'll play a tune on his ribs with my boot." He got up painfully and limped over toward his bike. "Now get out of here, both of you."

Joe turned and walked away, calling Mophead after him. They both had a hang-dog look as they slunk off down the street.

"Never mind, Mophead," Joe said quietly. "It was an accident. You couldn't really help it."

Mophead seemed to agree. He lifted his head as he walked along, watching Joe carefully with his two bright eyes.

"We'll go up to Uncle Harry's gas station. Would you like that? Maybe he's got something in the fridge in the office."

Mophead barked and wagged his tail enthusiastically. He didn't understand what Joe was suggesting, but it sounded promising. Of all the people in Cockle Bay, Joe was the only one willing to take an interest in him.

But as they approached the gas station, Joe could hear Uncle Harry arguing with someone in the office. It was a Mr. Harding from Port Lincoln who had lent Uncle Harry some money—probably to buy the garage or *Seahorse*, his boat—and now he wanted some of it back again. Uncle Harry was saying that he didn't have any money handy at the moment, and so Harding would have to wait for it. They were raising their voices more and more.

"You're a cheat," Harding shouted.

"And you're a Scrooge, a real skinflint."

"I'll have to foreclose, that's what. I have no alternative."

Joe slunk away with Mophead. He hated quarrels and arguments. He'd had quite enough of them even when he was still a little boy, listening to his mother and father bickering all the time. People always seemed to be fighting among themselves. It didn't say much for human beings and the way they lived.

"We'll go home and have a drink," Joe said. "I'm dying of thirst."

Although it was only ten o'clock in the morning, the sun was very hot and the light flared up from the surface of the limestone street. It was early in January, the beginning of summer, with not a cloud in the sky. Aunt Ellen was watering a few spindly potted plants on the front porch with a bucket and ladle. Joe gulped down two big glasses of cold water from a plastic jug in the fridge.

"Is there anything for Mophead?" he called. "Anything to eat?"

Aunt Ellen came to the door. "There are some old bones near the sink. You can give him a few if you like."

Mophead wagged his tail so much that there was a breeze all around him. Then he crouched down on his haunches with the bones between his front paws and chewed like a lion.

"I think I'll go down for a swim, Auntie," Joe said.

"Good idea, Joe. The girls are down there already."

Joe liked his aunt. She was a kind, happy person with a smiling face and little puckers near her eyes from a lifetime spent in the bright glinting sunlight.

He put on his trunks, draped a towel over his shoulders, and walked out the front door. Mophead finished chewing a last bit of meat from the bones, buried them hastily in the front garden, and loped off after Joe. Aunt Ellen watched them go.

"He's starting to follow you everywhere, that dog," she called. "You'll have to put a stop to it. We don't want him hanging around here all the time."

Joe didn't answer. He felt sad. Poor old Mophead was being chased away again. It was always the same, even with people. If you didn't have a place of your own, nobody wanted you. "Shove off," they said, "get lost, go someplace else."

It was more than three months since Joe had visited Wayward Island. Wayward Island was a desolate bit of land in the sea, twenty miles out past Cockle Bay. Uncle Harry leased it from its owner. In return for keeping an eye on the place, Uncle Harry was allowed to graze his five hundred sheep there. Once a year, in September, he spent a whole week shearing on the island. The island was a wild, beautiful place, and Joe had loved it the first time he saw it. Since then he'd only made one other trip there. He had been hoping desperately that the family would be able to spend a whole week on the island at Christmastime, but the plan had fallen through because Uncle Harry's service station had suddenly become very busy with tourists and vacationers. For Joe the days passed slowly and time was starting to drag. And it was hot. "Hot enough to fry eggs on your face," Herc Sampson, his uncle's helper on the boat, said. Joe found himself wishing more and more that they could all go over to Wayward Island and lie around every day with the cool sea breeze riffling through their hair.

He and Mophead ran across the road toward the dunes above the beach. Mophead barked excitedly in anticipation. He liked splashing in the water, and he especially liked chasing the colored beach ball the girls always played with.

"Come on," Joe shouted. "I'll race you."

They dashed off down the dunes, swerving past tussocks and plunging deep into the windblown drifts, sending the loose sand flying ahead of their feet like fine salt. Meg and Maureen were tossing the colored ball back and forth near the edge of the water. They looked up hastily as the boy and the dog came hurtling down the steep slope onto the flat stretch of the beach. Mophead won the race by an inch and then stood with his feet in the waves, barking wildly and happily.

"Ahh, why did you bring *him*?" Maureen asked. "He always rolls in the sand when he's wet and then shakes himself all over us."

"He's happy down here," Joe answered.

"He's as clumsy as a hippo. Dad says he's got five feet. He runs into people."

Joe laughed. "He ran into Porker Bacon this morning and knocked him clean off his bike."

"There you are, see. That's just what I said."

Meg was bouncing the ball up and down on the hard sand. Mophead stood nearby, waiting eagerly. Meg teased him. "What do you want, Mophead? Have you got ants under your toenails?"

Maureen was nine, and everyone said she was so small that she was only knee high to a centipede.

Meg looked twice as tall, even though she was only three years older. Her mother kept saying that she must have stood in a bag of fertilizer, because she was growing like a beanstalk. Meg often treated little Maureen badly, telling her she was a wimp and a stupid twit. Joe felt unhappy then, just as he did when Meg turned on him, too, and put him down in front of other people. Sometimes he wondered whether she realized how cruel she could be.

Meg and Joe were both twelve. They had been born on the same day, but they were not at all alike. She was tall and thin and he was short and mousy. Meg was capable and independent. Some of her friends found her overpowering. Joe was kind and good-natured, but his past life had made him shy.

"I'm going in to cool off," Joe said, throwing his towel on the beach. He turned to Mophead. "Come on, boy, come for a swim."

"I'm coming too," Meg said.

"Wait for me, wait for me," yelled Maureen.

All four of them raced into the water. Mophead jumped up and down over the waves, barking madly until he reached the deep water, where his legs weren't long enough to touch the sandy bottom anymore. Then he started to dog-paddle furiously, his nose thrust forward on the water like a crocodile's snout.

"Race you out to the deck," Meg called to Joe.

The "deck" was a flat-topped raft that was moored

thirty to forty yards out in the bay. It was a wonderful place for diving and jumping into the water or for lying like lizards in the sun.

"Wait for me, wait for me," spluttered Maureen as they swam. Meg was a strong swimmer. She reached the raft ahead of Joe and hung there for a second or two, catching her breath. Then they both turned to wait for Maureen and Mophead, who had to be helped onto the flat deck because they couldn't hoist themselves up on their own. Eventually they were all on board.

"It's beautiful out here," Meg said.

Joe agreed. "Yes, with just the three of us."

At that moment Mophead shook himself furiously and sent a shower of sharp little water drops over their arms and faces.

"With just the *four* of us," shrieked Maureen.

"Just three people," Meg said sourly, "and one big pest."

"There are people on the jetty," Maureen piped. "You have to count them too."

They all looked across the bay toward the jetty about a hundred yards away. A couple of fishing boats were moored against it, and some of the crewmen were moving about unloading fish or taking on supplies. Joe stood with his hands on his hips, squinting over the water. He already knew the boats and their skippers so well that he could have listed them with his eyes shut.

"Mick Mareolas and Greasy Bellamy on this side,"

he said, "and Tiny Mazerakis and Stewy Sampson on the other."

He turned his head slowly and looked out over the beach to the horizon. Cockle Bay really was a beautiful place. The tiny town was cupped in the curving shore, with the white beach in front of the tussocky dunes behind. At either end of the bay the crescent of sand ended in a low rocky headland that was almost surrounded by white breakers and green shallows. Between them ran the blue ribbon of the deeper channel that led out to the open sea. *Seahorse*, Uncle Harry's cutter, and one or two tuna boats were riding at their moorings just at the edge of it.

Joe took a deep breath. After Melbourne's constant racket this was the most peaceful place in the world. The jetty was like a long wooden millipede waddling out into the water on a thousand rickety legs. Its back looked gray and bony in the sun.

One of the fishermen started cleaning his catch of whiting. His knife glinted as he scaled and gutted the fish, and his arm jerked as he threw the offal overboard into the water. Sea gulls came streaming in for the feast until the sea was white with them—a confusion of bodies screaming and jostling madly.

They watched for a while, but Maureen couldn't stand still for long. She suddenly pinched her nose with her thumb and forefinger, took a quick run along the deck of the raft, and jumped as far as she could with her knees bent high in the air. She landed with a tremendous splash. A few moments later she was back, hanging on to the handholds and calling for someone to help her up. Then Meg and Joe joined in too, and after rushing about on the deck in a frenzy of excitement, even Mophead took a running jump and landed in the water with a thunderous splash.

"That's the biggest belly flopper of the day," Meg called.

Joe laughed and accidentally swallowed a mouthful of seawater. They leaped in and out for a while, tumbling and jostling. Twice Joe pretended to lose his balance and fell backward into the water like a clown. Maureen shrieked and coughed. Mophead barked wildly. It was some time before they settled down on the deck again, cringing away from Mophead whenever he shook himself all over the place like a sprinkler.

After a while Meg turned to Joe. "Let's have another race."

He was surprised. "Where to?"

"Over to the jetty. The first one to touch the wooden steps wins."

"Okay, but it's a fair distance."

"No it's not."

"First Maureen and Mophead will have to go back to the beach. We can't leave them here by themselves."

There was a howl of protest from Maureen and a great deal of reluctance from Mophead. The deadlock was finally broken when Joe and Meg agreed to wait until Maureen had dog-paddled ashore and run up to the jetty to act as judge. Mophead was persuaded to follow her after Joe had given him a mighty push that sent him flying through the air for the first two yards of his journey.

Eventually Meg and Joe lined up at the edge of the pontoon and waved to show that they were about to start.

"Ready?" Joe asked.

"Ready when you are."

"We'll go at the count of three. One . . . two . . . THREE!"

They hit the water together. Although Meg was a fast swimmer, Joe was hoping that he had more stamina and could catch up later in the race.

But Meg showed no signs of weakening. She was as lean and straight as an arrow, and she kept increasing her lead. Before long she was two yards ahead, then three, then four. By swimming desperately, Joe managed to hold her at that for a while as they passed the halfway mark, but by the time they had swum three quarters of the distance she had gone still farther ahead, and he could see that he had no hope of catching her. They were both tiring, gulping in great gasps of air and splashing raggedly.

Meg was within fifteen or twenty yards of the wooden steps that led down into the water from the jetty and Joe was five yards behind her when they heard a shout. As his head moved from side to side in the overarm action of his swimming, Joe raised his eyes—blurred by the water as they were— and saw three or four men rushing to the rail at the edge of the jetty, yelling and pointing. At first he thought they were cheering and urging him on, but then he sensed panic in their movements.

Instinctively he looked back and out of the corner of his eye glimpsed a shape, a long dark shape like a log or a torpedo coming up behind him. His numbed brain found the answer at exactly the same instant as he heard the cry from the jetty: "*Shark!*" He swung onto his side, looking back along his shoulder, frozen with fright.

At that moment Stewy Sampson, who had been cutting up a large stingray that had tangled itself in his nets during the night, seized a big piece of flap and hurled it over the jetty rail toward him. Luckily it fell with a great splash just behind Joe's body—between his threshing feet and the oncoming shark. It saved his life. The shark checked its forward rush, veered aside for a second or two, and then made for the piece of flesh. It swung over in a majestic half roll, opened its great jaws, and swallowed the chunk as if it had been a tiny morsel.

Stewy had given the swimmers a little breathing space. By the time the shark had wolfed down its tidbit, Meg had reached the steps and Joe was only five or six yards away. Stewy came rushing down, carrying another hunk of the stingray, judging the shark's movements. Again he hurled the flesh just beyond Joe.

"Swim, Joe," he bellowed. "Swim for your life."

Joe did. As he reached the steps, several pairs of hands seized him and yanked him hurriedly out of the water.

"Holy catfish," said Mick Mareolas, "that was close."

"Look, look." The others were peering and pointing. Joe and Meg turned. They were both as white as paper, their chests heaving and their breath panting, but they were in time to see the shark come in for its second helping.

"Look at the size of him," Mick said in awe. "He's an absolute monster."

Again the shark moved in its strange rolling action, almost breaking the surface as it opened its huge jaws. It was no more than the length of a fishing rod from the steps where they were all standing.

"Look," Meg cried. "He's got a scar all the way down in his face. See, on the top jaw."

The shark swept before them in a tight circle, almost like a circus animal expecting more meat at feeding time. Meg was right. A wavering white mark like an old crease ran down the shark's head. It started near the left eye and ended at the upper edge of his curving jaw.

"That's old Scarface," Stewy shouted. "He's back."

Mick raised his brows. "Scarface?"

"Sure. A fisherman slashed him once with a harpoon, years ago. Nobody has seen him for years. Thought he was dead."

Meg was peering over the edge, watching the shark cruise by. He was gigantic—seventeen to twenty feet long and ten or twelve feet around the girth. "Well, if he's dead," she said wryly, "I wouldn't like to meet him when he's alive."

The shark cruised about for a few minutes longer like a shadowy and terrifying missile under the water, and then turned sharply and disappeared. They all climbed slowly to the deck of the jetty. Joe turned to Stewy. "Thanks, Mr. Sampson. You saved me for sure." He was beginning to suffer from shock, and his teeth were chattering.

"No sweat, Joe," Stewy answered. "Lucky I had the ray handy." He looked at both of them critically. "You two had better go home and rest." He smiled. "I think I need a stiff brandy myself."

When Uncle Harry came home from work that night and heard about Scarface, he was angry. "It's those stupid fishermen," he said. "They ought to have their heads examined."

Joe looked up quickly. "Why, Uncle?"

"Because they feed the sharks."

Joe was open-mouthed. *"Feed* them?"

"Yes. They clean their fish on the jetty and throw the leftovers into the sea—fish heads, offal, the lot. And then they wonder why the sharks are suddenly back in the bay. If they cleaned their catches out on the fishing grounds, there'd be no problem."

"It's not only the fishermen," answered Aunt Ellen. "The locals do it too. And the tourists—the visitors and campers."

Uncle Harry munched loudly. "Well, whoever they are, they ought to be stopped. Soon the whole bay will be useless for swimming; it won't be safe to dip your big toe in the water. It makes my blood run cold to think of the three of you out there in the water with a shark like Scarface. He's big enough to bite a horse in half."

"The *four* of us," Joe said.

Uncle Harry puckered up his face. "What's that?"

"Not three. There were four of us. Mophead was with us too."

"That's even worse. Dogs attract sharks."

"But we don't really see many of them, do we?" Joe said. "There can't be many all together."

Uncle Harry spluttered. "Sharks? Not many of them? Good Lord, the place is teeming with sharks. They're as thick as anchovies."

Joe was depressed. "But not on the coast—only out in open water?"

"Everywhere, especially between here and the island. It's one of the best big-game spots in the world, if that's what you want."

"For sharks?"

"Yes."

Meg looked up with a grin. "You mean to say

that we sail over them every time we go out to the island?"

Her father knew she was teasing him. "Yes," he answered, "they know when you two are on board; they're looking for you just as Scarface was today."

"A sort of reception committee?" Meg was being a smart aleck.

Aunt Ellen had had enough. "That'll do, Margaret," she said sternly. "There's no need to be fresh about it. A shark attack is not a thing to joke about. Have you stopped to imagine what could have happened out there in the bay today? Have you?"

Meg hung her head. "No, Mom, not really."

"Well, just think about it, really think about it. And then finish your tea."

2

In the middle of January, Meg and Maureen went to Port Lincoln to spend a few weeks' holiday with friends. It was a long trip, and although they telephoned to say they had arrived safely, they seemed to be at the other end of the world.

Joe was desperately lonely. He missed Meg especially. Even though she could sometimes sting like a wasp, she was full of fun. And she was a leader. If there were jobs to be done, she was always the first to finish. If they had time on their hands, she was the one with a dozen ideas. If they were just talking, she seemed to know so many things—not only about her schoolwork but about the sea and the coastline, about animals and trees and the country inland, even about ropes and knots and navigating the cutter under the stars. The place was not the same without her.

Joe stood on the hill behind Uncle Harry's house, looking down at the little town spread-eagled around him. It really was a dump: a few shops scattered here and there along the street with overgrown land between, a couple of forlorn churches, a dilapidated hall that needed painting, one hotel, Uncle Harry's garage, an old rusty wharf shed near the jetty, and a few dozen houses that looked as if they'd been dropped there by accident.

At the edge of the town stood the school—an Area School, it was called—where he had learned to mix with a hundred or more children from the town, from the farms, and from fishermen's shacks up and down the coast. Behind him there were nothing but limestone plains, bare paddocks, and drooping mallee trees. On either side the coast stretched far away in the heat haze—northwest toward Ceduna and the head of the Great Bight, southeast toward Port Lincoln and Cape Catastrophe. And straight ahead, as Joe shifted his gaze southward, was the curving shore of the little bay and beyond that the vast plain of the sea glinting in the glare of the sun.

It was incredible, Joe thought to himself. After Melbourne, the loneliness was enough to make a person crazy. The silence was suffocating, the solitude maddening. He had an urge to yell at the top of his voice: "Hello, is anyone still alive in the world? Is there still a penguin in Antarctica who can hear me?" But then he saw Porker Bacon wobbling down the street on his bike toward the hotel, and he knew that all human life was not yet extinct.

Deep down he was unhappy. It was all really because of what had happened in Melbourne. His mother had gone away years before, and obviously she was not interested in him anymore. He didn't even know where she was or whether she was still alive. His father had been very good to him, but then he had started to get ill. It had gone on and on, getting worse and worse, until he had died of cancer. His friends had all clicked their tongues. "Such a young, strong man. Only thirty-five, still in the prime of his life." And so Uncle Harry and Aunt Ellen, who had come for the funeral, had suggested to Joe that he should go back to Cockle Bay with them. "You'll be just like one of the family, Joe."

But Joe knew that he wasn't one of the family. Although his uncle and aunt were wonderfully good to him, he was an outsider, an added burden, an extra mouth to feed. He knew it more certainly than ever a few nights later, when he heard Uncle Harry talking to Aunt Ellen about the money they owed to Mr. Harding.

"He's threatening us now, you know. If we don't pay up, he says he'll repossess. He's got troubles too. They say he's lost a lot of money in his building business and has big commitments of his own to meet."

Joe's ears burned. He wasn't sure what "repossess" meant, but he guessed that something was going to be taken away. It would have to be *Seahorse*. And what would Uncle Harry do without a boat? He would have to give up Wayward Island altogether. He would have to lose the sheep.

Joe moped about moodily for days after that. He even wondered whether he should run away so that they wouldn't have the expense of keeping him anymore. Uncle Harry was aware of Joe's loneliness and tried to do something about it. He took him for rides in his old truck whenever he went out delivering barrels of gas or oil to the farmers, and he used him as a helper in the garage if there was a broken tow bar to weld or a worn-out engine to fix.

Sometimes Joe worked the pump and served impatient drivers with gas, but he had to be careful not to offend old Otto Minz, who was Uncle Harry's "official" assistant. Otto was a retired farmer who lived alone in a small house near the garage. He was a huge man, with an untidy crop of hair that looked like straw from a packing case and a big red nose like the blunt end of a carrot. He arrived punctually each morning and sat on a stool beside the gas pump to prevent Uncle Harry from being interrupted when he was busy in the workshop.

Old Otto knew every person within thirty miles

of Cockle Bay, so he was able to exchange all the news of the district with his customers. When a stranger pulled up for gas, Otto stood questioning the driver for a long time before starting to fill the tank. He usually wanted to know the stranger's name, where he had come from, where he was going, why he was making the trip, how long it would take, how much gas his car was using, how many people there were in his family, and whether he liked the summer heat. He would then pass on this information to the next customer, together with a few guesses and imaginings of his own.

It was clear, therefore, that Joe had to be very careful not to rob old Otto of this important service to the district, and so if there was nothing for him to do in the workshop, he usually went off to play with Mophead and his slimy tennis ball. The two of them were playing near the hotel corner one morning when Boxhead Sampson came striding up from the jetty. Boxhead was Herc's younger brother—a big fellow of sixteen who worked on the fishing boat with his father, Stewy. The sides and the top of his head were so straight that it was easy to see how he had earned his nickname.

"Dad wonders whether you'd like to come fishin'," Boxhead said. "I've seen Harry Blake, and he says it's okay if you want to."

It took Joe a second or two to figure out that Harry Blake was his uncle Harry. Then his face lit up ecstatically. "Would I ever? Gee, thanks."

"Get your things then; we're leaving in half an hour. We should be back by tonight or tomorrow morning at the latest. Just have to get some table fish for the pub."

Joe tore off even before Boxhead had finished. Mophead couldn't understand what the excitement was about, but he followed happily all the way home, just in case it involved bones or meat scraps. Aunt Ellen smiled at Joe. "Steady, steady," she said, "or you'll burst your boiler."

"I have to hurry. They're leaving in twenty minutes."

"Slow down and pack your things."

"I don't need much."

"Take your sunglasses and your old army hat— the one with the wide brim." She took a tube of sunburn cream from the kitchen and handed it to him. "And take this too."

He wrinkled his nose. "I don't need that, Auntie. I'm as brown as anything."

"Take it," she said firmly, "and put some on your lips and face right away."

"Do I have to?"

"Yes. Don't try to tell your old aunt how to live in Cockle Bay. The sun will be vicious out there. The glare from the water will strike up into your face. There'll be salt on your lips. If you're not very careful, you'll come home looking like a lump of corned beef."

He hung his head and did as he was told.

"Take a spare pair of jeans in case you get wet," she added. "And a pair of sneakers. You can't fish in bare feet—not with hooks of all kinds flying about. And you'd better take an old sweater."

He recoiled. "A sweater? Gee, it's a hundred degrees outside."

"It can get very cold at night, especially if the wind comes up."

At last he was ready. She smiled as he made for the door. "Good-bye, Joe. Have a good time."

"Sure. Thanks Aunt Ellen."

She was going to say something more, but he was already out of earshot, racing down the slope toward the jetty with Mophead careering after him.

She sighed. Boys, she decided, were just as impatient as girls.

Stewart Sampson's boat was *Petrel,* a solid old thing that had seen better days but that still had a lot of life left in her—or so Stewy said. They made for Herringbone Shoal, a few miles southwest of Cockle Bay. It was a place that gave sea captains nightmares because it was full of dangers for big ships—reefs and rocks, sandbars and shallows, and deepwater channels that ended in shoals without warning. But the fishermen loved it. There were so many rocky grottoes, so many weedy hollows and sand patches where fish teemed—snapper and whiting and trevally and gar and a dozen varieties more—

that the people of Cockle Bay had a kind of private fish farm right at their front door.

Stewy brought *Petrel* down the sheltered side of the shoal until he reached one of his favorite spots. Then he cut the motor and drifted for a minute or two, peering intently over the port side. Boxhead let the anchor go and waited until the flukes had gripped. "Okay," he called, picking up his gear. "Shall I warn the fish you're here, Joe?" He pulled out a bucket of bait. "Try for whiting; it's too late in the day for snapper."

Stewy came down from the wheelhouse and joined them. Within ten seconds of casting out his line he had the first bite, and a moment or two later hauled in a big whiting. It came up out of the sea with water falling from it in shining drops—a lovely fish, speckled and brown and golden. Stewy grabbed it by the head, twisted it free, and tossed it into the well, where it darted off and swam around and around as if astonished at the sudden change in its environment. A second later Boxhead hauled in another one, and then Joe pulled in a third.

"Whee," Stewy called jubilantly. "They've found us today."

Joe looked up. "I thought *we* found *them*."

Stewy laughed. "That's what people like to think. But there's so much water mixed up with the fish that we're helpless unless they come to us."

They fished steadily for an hour or more. Then, when the biting began to slacken, they moved farther down the shoal to another spot that proved to be even better.

By lunchtime Joe was exultant. He had caught almost thirty on his own, and Stewy and Boxhead had landed more than ten dozen between them. The well was crowded with a jostling mass of fish.

Stewy stood upright slowly and bent his body forward and backward three or four times. "Oh, my squeaking bones," he said. "They need oiling." Then he stood wiping his hands on an old cloth, smiling at Joe, who still was casting out eagerly.

"Haul in, my hearties," he called. "Time for lunch."

He threw down the cloth and stood rubbing his hands up and down his dirty overalls in a final effort to get himself clean and dry.

"Come on, Joe," he said. "We've got something good down below—hot coffee, sandwiches and chocolate cake." Joe reeled in his line and followed him down. It wasn't until he was sitting there next to Boxhead that he suddenly felt his face burning. He touched it gingerly. Stewy saw him and laughed.

"Just as well you put some cream on your nose. Your face is all lit up. We could stand you up on the headland and use you instead of the lighthouse."

Joe blushed, but it didn't show. Even his freckles seemed to have blended into his fiery skin.

When they came up after lunch they saw another boat about half a mile away—a small fiberglass motorboat with an outboard motor. It was anchored not far from a rocky outcrop on the edge of Herringbone Shoal.

"They're trying for snapper," said Boxhead. "They must be campers."

Stewy stood with his big legs apart and his hips braced against the rail, peering at the strange boat through his binoculars. "They ought to be locked up," he said, "coming out here in a thing like that."

"Too small?" Joe asked.

"Too small and too flimsy. Things can get pretty rough out here—big seas, rips, white water. They'd be flipped over like a ten-cent piece."

"Who's in it?" Boxhead asked.

"Two guys. Must be visitors, all right. Nobody owns a boat like that around here." Stewy turned to Boxhead. "Pull up the anchor. We'll drift down toward them for a while and then head for home."

As they drew nearer to the other boat, they could see some kind of commotion going on. One man, who had been pulling up his line, started to leap about wildly, and the other one seized an oar and prodded frantically at the water.

Boxhead chuckled. "Sharks," he said. "They've got those two fellows stirred up like a hornets' nest."

Joe was amazed. "How do you know that?"

Boxhead was laughing out loud. "It's easy enough to read the signs. If you've got a fish on your line, the sharks follow it up. They tear it off while you're pulling, or just bite it in half."

He took the binoculars from his father and stood watching. Then he laughed again. "One fellow's just pulled in a big fish head. Not a fish, just the head. They must be getting a few snapper after all." He peered intently. "The first guy is as mad as a hornet over it. I'll bet he's got steam coming out of his ears."

Stewy was watching near the wheelhouse. "The other fellow's trying to bash the shark with an oar," he said. "It must be following the line right up to the surface."

"They'll fall overboard in a minute if they keep that up," Stewy added as they drifted nearer. "Then we'll really see a circus."

Just then the first man jerked his line again as if he had hooked another fish, and then started to haul it in frantically. His companion stood beside him with the oar upraised. Judging by the actions of both men, it seemed to be a desperate race.

Boxhead chuckled excitedly, his eyes pressed to the binoculars. "He's sure trying to beat the shark this time," he called. "He's winding like a dynamo."

And then, as they all watched intently, an amazing thing happened. The angler, leading in the race to get his catch on board ahead of the shark, heaved wildly and hauled the fish all the way out of the sea in a swift smooth arc. At the same instant a huge shark, coming up from below at high speed, broke the surface in pursuit—and shot up out of the water for almost half its own length. There was a split second of awe and stunned silence.

"Holy Moses," said Stewy.

The shark had not come up vertically but at an angle, within a yard of the fiberglass hull, and so instead of falling back the way it had come, it fell forward as its impetus carried it on. About a third of its length came down across the stern of the boat. It was as if two tons of concrete had suddenly been dropped on the boat from above. The great bulk of the shark smashed the transom, stove in the hull, and forced the stern under the water. At the same time the bow reared up and pointed at the sky. The two men were hurled backward into the sea, and the whole boat slid out of sight as quickly and smoothly as someone going down a slippery slide.

"Oh my gosh."

Joe had barely finished his exclamation when Stewy sprang forward to the wheelhouse. The next moment the engine roared and the throttle went over to "full speed ahead." As the propeller gripped hard, *Petrel* lifted her bow and plunged off toward the spot where the boat had gone down. It was all so sudden that Joe fell over in a heap. By the time he could get to his feet again, the cutter was already halfway to the fishermen, charging across the sea like a destroyer.

"Grab the boathook," Stewy yelled to Boxhead. "And have a lifebuoy ready."

Luckily the two men from the motorboat could

swim. They were threshing about, waving wildly and trying to yell between gulps and splutters. Stewy swung *Petrel* broadside on and cut the engine. "Quick," he shouted. "Grab their arms and help them aboard." There was a minute of confusion, a chaotic jumble of slipping fingers and clutching hands, of splashes and thumps, scrabbles and scratches, cries and grunts. But finally they managed to haul both men aboard over the stern, where they stood with water streaming from their clothes onto the soaked duckboard beneath.

"Thanks," panted the first man. "Thanks."

"You're lifesavers," croaked the second. "I thought we were goners."

He took off his wet jacket and dropped it on the deck. It fell with a flop, like a wet dishcloth. "Did you see the size of him—that shark? I thought my legs were going to be torn off at any minute."

The first man shuddered. There were goose bumps all the way down his arm. "I don't even know what sort he was."

"A white pointer," Stewy answered. "A big white pointer. We've got lots of 'em around here. Huge fellows—one ton, two tons, maybe even three tons."

"No wonder he sank the boat."

"Your boat was far too small for these waters," Stewy said. "Lucky we were here. You would have been drowned."

"Or eaten alive."

"One thing," said the second man. "We'll always

be able to recognize the brute if we ever meet him again."

"Who wants to?" said his companion.

"Why?" asked Stewy. "Why would you recognize him?"

"He's got a big scar on his face. It's as clear as a road map. A white mark."

Joe drew in his breath sharply. "It's *him*," he said softly.

The men were puzzled. "What did you say?"

Stewy went back to the wheelhouse and started the engine. "Scarface," he said quietly. "Scarface Bill. He's a legend around here. And we haven't seen the last of him."

The two men stood talking to Stewy all the way back to Cockle Bay. Joe sat nearby, listening eagerly to everything that was going on. One of the men had red hair, and his companion called him Carrottop. He seemed to do most of the talking.

"Any hope of salvaging our boat?" he asked Stewy.

"Not a chance. It's a write-off."

"The water's not very deep, is it?"

"No."

"I'd like to save the outboard if I could. It's brand-new."

"Can you dive—with scuba gear?"

"Not really."

"Well, you wouldn't get the locals to go down for you. Not here."

"Why not?"

"Too dangerous. Rips and currents, crazy tides, white water. And sharks."

Carrottop nodded. "Yes, sharks."

"They love the reef," Stewy said. "It's a good place for food. They'll pick up anything—baby seals, fish, injured porpoises, other sea creatures, offal . . ."

"And people," Carrottop added wryly.

"Sometimes—especially people who splash about wildly in a panic. They can sense panic like magic."

The flesh on Joe's neck suddenly prickled with goose bumps. In his mind's eye he could see Scarface again, coming up behind him in Cockle Bay as he and Meg were trying to reach the steps of the town jetty. It was a picture he saw only too often, in nightmares when he was asleep and in flashbacks when he was awake.

"They're all white pointers, are they?" Carrottop asked.

"Mostly. We've got some of the biggest pointers in the world around here. They're magnificent fellows. Majestic. Awe-inspiring."

"How long do they live?"

"We don't know. Old Scarface has been around for thirty years or more, but heaven knows how old he really is. He could be a hundred."

"Do they get any bigger than Scarface?"

"Oh yes. The fishermen here have seen some huge chaps. Absolute monsters. Twenty or twenty-five feet long. Must weight three or four tons."

Carrottop's companion rolled his eyes. "I think we'll leave the boat and the outboard where they are."

"I would." Stewy pushed his hat back and scratched his head. "The really big fellows are sly and shrewd. They've lived a long time and they've learned a lot. They tend to keep to themselves. They like broken water and shadows because they provide a sort of camouflage. But they'll come into the open if they're really hungry."

"Like Scarface?"

"Well, now and again you get one that starts making a real nuisance of himself—a sort of rogue shark. Hangs about the bay, cruises near the jetty, follows the boats. In the end he becomes a pest."

"A dangerous pest," Carrottop added.

"If he gets too bad, we have to get rid of him."

"Like Scarface?"

"Like Scarface."

3

There was a hubbub of discussion at the tea table that night. Uncle Harry and Aunt Ellen were both wide-eyed at Joe's story about Scarface and the way he had sunk the fishermen's runabout. Uncle Harry was particularly interested in the description of the men.

"Good heavens," he said. "I served those two fellows yesterday. They wanted fuel for the outboard."

"One had red hair," Joe said. "The other one called him Carrots or Carrottop."

"That's right. He was towing the boat on a trailer. I pointed to it and said, 'How far out are you going in that thing?' and he answered, 'Out to Herringbone Shoal.' So I looked at him and said, 'Well, you'll end up as shark bait if you do.' He was a bit uppity about it. He didn't want to believe me."

Joe laughed. "He would have believed you when we fished him out of the sea after Scarface jumped into his boat."

Aunt Ellen clicked her tongue. "It must have been an awful thing to see."

"It frightened everyone, even Boxhead."

"And to think it was the same shark."

Uncle Harry dunked a cracker in his cup of tea. "That's what worries me. I think Scarface is going to hang around for a long time now."

Aunt Ellen pushed the crumbs together on her plate with a knife. "They come three times, and the third time is always the worst. That's what people say."

Uncle Harry snorted. "That's a lot of superstitious rot."

Joe fidgeted. "But he does seem to like this spot, doesn't he?"

"Naturally, if people keep throwing food into the bay. He won't show up just three times, though. He'll be here ten times, twenty times, a hundred times. He'll be here all day and every day. We'll have to put up a sign on the beach: THIS BAY IS SHARK INFESTED. COME AND ENJOY A SWIM WITH SCARFACE. That'll be a nice advertisement for the town."

Uncle Harry was so critical of the fishermen that

Joe was worried. He could see an argument developing, splitting people into two camps. If that happened, he didn't want his uncle to be on one side and Stewy and Boxhead on the other.

In bed that night he had a terrifying dream about a huge shark that arched itself up like a porpoise and crashed right through the side of *Petrel* while they were out fishing at the Herringbone Shoal. The sea poured in as he struggled to get out of his bunk, threshing furiously with his arms and legs. The water was as thick as molasses, twining itself around his hands and holding him back. His lungs were fit to burst. Then, to his horror, he saw that the shark was actually in the boat, opening its cavernous jaws within a yard of his head. He recoiled sideways and felt a stinging pain near his temple as he crashed against the splintered timbers in his frenzy to escape. Mercifully, he woke up then. The sheets were twisted around his arms from his frantic swimming in bed, and his forehead was throbbing from the blow he had given it when he had flung himself against the bedside dresser to avoid the shark.

"Moses," he said to himself as he slowly collected his wits. "If this keeps up, I'll have sharks swimming up the main street and stopping for gas at Uncle Harry's service station."

The next morning Mophead was waiting for Joe on the front verandah. Aunt Ellen eyed both of them sternly. "Really, Joe," she said, "I thought I told you—"

"I'm sorry, Aunt," Joe broke in, "but he just follows me everywhere."

"Obviously."

"I think he likes me."

She raised her eyes to heaven. "Who would have guessed?"

"There's nothing I can do about it."

"It's what you've already done that's the problem. You're always playing with him."

"Well, someone has to be kind to him. Nobody else wants him."

"Exactly."

Mophead sat watching them intently, as if he knew that he was the center of discussion. His dark eyes shone brightly like big polished buttons, and his mouth seemed to be shaping itself into a friendly grin. He stood up, took a step forward, and wagged his tail.

"He . . . he sort of thinks he belongs to me."

She sighed wearily. "Look, I'm sorry, Joe, but we can't afford to keep a dog. We really can't."

"I could catch rabbits for him."

"Don't be silly. You wouldn't have enough time after school. And the drought has killed off most of the rabbits anyway."

"I could catch fish then."

She turned to go inside. "It's out of the question, Joe." The door closed behind her with a snap.

Joe looked at Mophead sadly. "I'm sorry, Mophead," he said. "It's not your fault." He looked out over the bay and the lonely sea beyond. "And it's not my fault either. It's just . . . it's just one of those things."

Mophead moved forward and licked Joe's hand. Then he sat on his haunches looking up wide-eyed, brushing the cement floor vigorously from side to side with his tail.

"Tell you what," Joe said. "Let's go down to Charlie Chops. He's your only hope."

Charlie Chops was actually Charles Cutter, the butcher. Everyone thought that Cutter was an unbelievable name for a butcher. Long ago someone had changed it to Chopper, and a little later this had been shortened to Chops. Now all the local people used it so automatically that half of them didn't even know his real name.

Mophead raced on ahead. He knew the name "Charlie Chops" so well that his mouth started to drool as soon as he heard it. When they arrived, Charlie was just opening up the shop, tying a striped apron around his big stomach. "Hah," he said cheerfully, looking at Mophead. "Here comes my best customer."

"I think he's hungry," Joe ventured.

Charlie roared. "Think? He's a canine vacuum cleaner."

"If it weren't for you, he'd starve."

Mophead stood expectantly through all this,

dripping little strings of saliva onto the sidewalk.
"All right then," Charlie said, and disappeared
into the back of the shop. A minute later he returned with some meaty flaps and a big leg bone.
Mophead gobbled up the meat and then hunched
himself over the bone in the middle of the street,
chewing relentlessly. Charlie watched him for a
while.

"Joe," he said suddenly, "does that dog of yours
obey you?"

"Don't call him my dog," Joe answered in alarm.
"Aunt Ellen would have a fit if she heard you."

"He behaves as if he's your dog."

"I know. That's the trouble."

"But would he do what you told him?"

"I think so. Why?"

Instead of answering directly, Charlie pointed
at the small truck standing behind the shop. Joe
knew that he used it from time to time to pick up
a few head of cattle or sheep that he later butch-
ered in his own slaughterhouse a mile or so out
of town. His wife tended the shop while he was
away.

"I have to go inland today," he said, "to fetch a
dozen sheep." In Cockle Bay "inland" meant any
place that was more than a stone's throw from the
coast. Joe waited for him to continue. "They're down
at Herbie Driver's place, but Herbie isn't home and
he's taken his dogs with him."

Joe was beginning to get the picture.

"I'm too old and fat," Charlie said, "to be rounding up the sheep on foot."

Joe smiled at the thought. "So?"

"So I was wondering about you and the dog."

Joe was delighted. "Sure. We can give him a try. But he's not a sheepdog, you know."

Charlie Chops guffawed so loudly that his big belly rollicked. "No, he's certainly not a sheepdog. He looks more like a sheep!"

Joe blushed for Mophead. "But he's very good-natured."

"He'll need to be. We can't have him roaring about after the rest of the flock, or Herbie'll come after us with a gun."

"What do you want him to do exactly?"

"Help yard the slaughterhouse sheep. If he just does what you tell him to do, he'll be a big help—keeping a bit of pressure on the sheep until they're in the yard."

"Okay, I'll ask Aunt Ellen if we . . ." He paused and corrected himself. "If I can come."

Mophead exceeded all expectations. It turned out that he had a natural way with sheep and he enjoyed the work immensely. Joe and Charlie used very simple commands: "Stay," Joe said every now and then, or "Go," or "Steady," or "Back, Mophead, back." Mophead did the rest by himself. Joe

· 41 ·

was sure that he must have had some experience with sheep when he was still a pup.

Charlie Chops was impressed. "Train him up just a little bit more and you'll be able to sell him for a very good price."

Joe put an arm around Mophead's neck. "He's not for sale, and he never will be."

"I'll make a bargain with you," Charlie said suddenly. "You sweep out the shop for me every day after school, and let me use the dog sometimes when I need him . . ."

Joe waited expectantly. "Yes?"

"Then in return I'll give you enough meat and scraps to feed him every night."

Joe couldn't believe his ears. "Every night? All through the year?"

"Yes, every night."

"Whee!" Joe was racing up the street before Charlie had finished speaking.

Aunt Ellen wasn't at home. He guessed that she had probably walked up to the garage, so he changed direction and ran up the hill. Mophead ran exuberantly at his heels.

"Aunt Ellen," Joe yelled. "Aunt Ellen, Uncle Harry."

They both came out of the workshop and watched him running toward them. "Can I keep Mophead if Charlie Chops feeds him?" He stood before them at last, panting hard. "Can I? Please?"

Aunt Ellen opened her mouth but then shut it

again without saying anything. Uncle Harry cleared his throat. "Is this the truth, Joe? Did Charlie say so?"

"Yes, yes. He suggested it. We made a bargain."

Aunt Ellen found her voice. "What sort of bargain?" she asked suspiciously.

"He'll give me the meat if I sweep out the shop—and if he can use Mophead sometimes."

"Use him? Whatever for?

"For the sheep. He's really good."

Uncle Harry snorted impatiently. "With sheep? He'd be like an elephant rounding up chickens."

"No, he's good. He must have lived on a farm once."

"Baloney. I'll bet he's never worked a sheep in his life."

"He has. He did today—out at Driver's place." Joe's eyes were shining. "And he'll get better and better with a bit of practice. We could even take him over to Wayward Island."

Uncle Harry's mouth opened in disbelief. "Wayward Island?"

"Yes. He'll save you a lot of walking. He's just like an old English sheepdog."

Aunt Ellen hardened her heart. "Joe, I thought I told you this morning—"

"But that was before Charlie's promise. We couldn't afford the food for him then but we *can* now."

Aunt Ellen lifted her right hand and then let it

fall helplessly at her side. "Oh, what's the use?" she said.

Uncle Harry smiled. "It looks like a *fait accompli*, don't you think?"

Joe didn't know what a *fait accompli* was—and he didn't like the sound of it. "Does it mean I can keep him then?"

"Ask your aunt."

Joe turned hastily. "Can I, Auntie?" He put on his most wheedling expression. "Please?"

She sighed resignedly. "Oh, I guess so Joe, if Charlie has promised the food."

He moved forward impulsively. For a moment she thought he was going to throw his arms around her neck and kiss her, but his past life had driven that sort of thing out of him years before. Instead he seized her by the hands and pressed them hard. "Thank you, Aunt Ellen. Thank you very much."

He turned and went rocketing back to Charlie with the news. Uncle Harry shouted after him. "Sweeping the shop will be a real job, Joe. Think about it. You'll have to keep up your end of the bargain."

Joe spun around briefly. "I will, I will. And I'll really look after Mophead. You'll see."

When Uncle Harry turned to look at Aunt Ellen, she had tears in her eyes. He smiled. "What's the matter, love?"

She wiped her eyes with the back of her hand.

"That boy," she said quietly, "and that dog. They really get to me sometimes."

The following day several families of vacationers came lumbering into Cockle Bay in their trailers. There were seven or eight children, half a dozen grown-ups, and two dogs. They bought groceries at the general store, beer at the Commercial Hotel, and gas at Uncle Harry's service station—after Otto Minz had cross-examined them closely. Then for the next two or three days they spent most of their time lounging and frolicking on the beach.

Joe went down to warn them soon after their arrival. "Don't go out into the deep water," he said, "and don't splash about too much. There are sharks." But they were a rough and rowdy lot and they refused to take him seriously.

"Phooey," one woman said. "We've come all the way up the coast and we haven't seen a shark yet. Not one."

"They're hard to see," Joe answered, "especially on cloudy days."

A man with a beer belly and a bald head made fun of him. "Look, son, any shark would be scared out of his wits at the sight of me. One glimpse, and he'd go for his life."

A skinny pimply fellow agreed. "Me too," he said, grinning stupidly. "I'm a terrible sight at any time, but I'm even worse in my swimming trunks."

On the second day all the visitors were in the water. They were fooling about, pushing one another under, dunking the dogs, and shrieking and splashing. Joe and Mophead were standing near the end of the jetty watching Mick Mareolas trundling a load of fish on the trolly.

Suddenly a helicopter swept in over the town with a noisy clatter, dipped toward the beach, and flew around in a wide circle. The children jumped up excitedly. "A helichopper, a helichopper," one of them yelled.

Cockle Bay had never seen anything like it before. "What's he doing in a place like this?" Mick asked.

"It must be from the oil rig out at sea," Joe answered. "I heard about it on the radio this morning. They had to bring a man in to the hospital at Ceduna."

"But what's he doing here?"

"Don't know. Must be on his way back to the rig."

But it didn't take long for them to find out. The helicopter circled the bay a second time and then, to their astonishment, came in and hovered above the open patch of land beyond the head of the jetty. Then it started to descend carefully right in front of their eyes.

"It's going to land," shrieked one of the little girls.

There was a moment of chaos—a roaring din and

a storm of dust and debris from the rotors—and the machine was rocking gently on the ground like a huge dragonfly.

"Good day," said the pilot cheerily as the children rushed toward him. All the others—the townspeople, the fishermen on the jetty, and the tourists on the beach—hurried forward inquisitively to see what it was all about.

"Thought I should just warn you," the pilot said, smiling. "You've got a visitor in the bay."

For a second Joe didn't understand the message. "A what?"

"A Charlie Ark. A real beauty. One of the biggest I've seen."

The news finally sank in. "Oh, a *shark*." The word seemed to echo raggedly down the line of the people toward those who were still coming up: *A shark . . . shark . . . shark. Big shark. In the bay. A shark.*

"He was swimming up the deepwater channel into the bay," the pilot went on. "That's when I first spotted him. Very bold and sure of himself he seemed."

The pilot turned to the campers who were just straggling up from the beach. "I wouldn't go back in the water if I were you. Not with that fellow in the bay. He was big enough to swallow an ox."

Joe glanced about quickly. Everyone was crowding toward the pilot, jostling and asking questions. Joe backed away cautiously and slipped off unnoticed. Within a second or two he was running bare-footed down the deck of the jetty toward the far end. But when he reached it, there was nothing unusual to be seen.

As he peered ugently from side to side, hoping for a glimpse of the monster, Mick Mareolas came back and started to clean up. He flushed the deck with a couple of buckets of seawater and gathered up various scraps.

"What are you looking for, Joe?" he asked jovially. "Mermaids?"

"The shark, but I can't see him."

Mick laughed. "Sharks are like ghosts. They're everywhere and nowhere."

"The helicopter pilot saw this one all right."

"By now he could be anywhere. He could have turned back, frightened by the shadow of the chopper or the vibrations." Mick seized a handful of offal and tossed it over the side. The pieces lay on the surface for a second or two and started to sink slowly. "The only thing that's predictable about sharks is that they're unpredictable."

Joe was about to turn and go back when he saw a movement in the water. He grabbed Mick's arm and pointed. "Look. Look there."

"Where?"

"There."

"Oh yes. Yes, I see him. Gosh, look at the size of him."

They watched, fascinated, as the great fish swam

toward them. Although they were seventy or a hundred feet away they could see his outline very clearly, because they were looking down on him from above. Suddenly he accelerated toward the pieces of fish until he was almost directly below them. He opened his huge jaws, and for an instant Joe saw the terrifying triangular teeth shining through the water. It was like a melting image on film, a watery glimpse through a window in the rain. Then the jaws closed and the dark shape of the shark was receding into deeper water.

"Did you see that?" Mick asked excitedly. "Did you see his face?"

"Not really."

"Well I did. The white line was there all right."

"Scarface?"

"Scarface, sure as death."

"Holy mackerel," said Joe. "He's back for sure."

When Uncle Harry heard about it later that day, he was very angry. "That's it," he said brusquely. "We'll have to do something now."

"What?" Joe asked.

"Get rid of him—before there's a real tragedy."

"How?"

"First we'll have to call a meeting in the hall, and then we'll invite someone over from Adelaide. Someone like George Lane."

"Who's George Lane?"

Uncle Harry smiled knowingly. "You could say

he's a specialist, Joe. A sort of professional shark remover."

During the next few days Joe learned a lot about George Lane. He was one of the best big-game fishermen in the world. He held five records, and he could tell more hair-raising stories about sharks than anyone else in Australia.

At the meeting, everyone agreed that George should be invited to Cockle Bay to try to catch Scarface. Uncle Harry even offered *Seahorse* free of charge provided the people of the town were willing to supply the gasoline. They all hoped George Lane would be prepared to pay his own fares and expenses.

Mick Mareolas thanked Uncle Harry and suggested that a barbecue should be held on the beach to pay for the gas and some of his lost time. Half a dozen people cried, "I second that," and there was a good deal of clapping and cheering.

When Meg and Maureen returned from Port Lincoln, Joe's spirits rose again. The house was a livelier place as soon as they walked through the door. Moreover, Meg was agog at the stories about Scarface and the wrecked motorboat and the helicopter and Mophead's success. It made Joe feel important.

The barbecue was held on the following Sunday. It would have been a wonderfully happy day for Joe if Mophead hadn't disgraced himself again. People began arriving long before noon. Soon the area near the head of the jetty and the approach roads on either side were full of parked cars, pickup trucks and trailers. People in shorts and bathing suits lounged in the shade of the jetty or set up colored beach umbrellas on the sand. Children raced in and out of the water. Men struggled down the slope with coolers, kegs, and cartons, women arranged blankets and baskets, and Charlie Chops and Stewy Sampson—the official cooks for the day— stood like stokers amid the swirling smoke and sizzling fat, manipulating sausages and chops with long-handled forks.

Mophead took advantage of the smoke and bustle and human preoccupation. Immediately behind Charlie and Stewy two bridge tables had been set up loaded with meat—mountains of chops and sausages. Coming from behind, Mophead found it easy to make a selection and then retire quietly into the tussocks above the highwater mark for lunch. As soon as he had finished he returned for a second serving, and then a third. By the time he was ready for a fourth helping he was becoming very selective, and so he ran his nose over the whole range of chops and along the loops of sausages to choose the best pieces.

It was his undoing. Leaning far forward to get a good sniff along the top of the meaty ridge, he accidentally pressed his heavy body against the leg of the bridge table. It collapsed spectacularly, catapulting the meat into the sand and suddenly bringing Mophead eyeball to eyeball with Stewy Sampson. A terrible sense of outrage was printed on Stewy's face. He raised his great fork like Neptune's trident and rushed at Mophead. "Damned dog," he roared. "I'll murder you, you thieving mongrel."

Mophead reeled back, spun around clumsily, and plunged off, scattering sand over the remaining table in his haste. The prongs of Stewy's fork darted after him and just managed to prick him in the rump. He yelped in panic. The next moment he was speeding away along the beach, with Stewy in pursuit yelling the most fearful vengeance.

Joe, Meg, and Nicky Reggio were building a sand castle for Maureen a few yards farther on. They had almost finished and were preparing to put turrets on the battlements when something like a hairy cannonball hurtled between them and demolished the whole castle. There were anguished cries on all sides.

"Hey, watch what you're doing."

"Get out."

"Stupid jerk."

"MOPHEAD!"

A second later Stewy Sampson was towering over them, breathing heavily, still brandishing his fork.

"That dog of yours," he roared at Joe. "That rotten, lousy, thievin' mutt. He's ruined half the meat."

Joe sprang to his feet. "Gee, I'm sorry, Mr. Sampson."

"So am I, the useless bum."

"I'll . . . I'll go and get him."

Stewy glared. "You do that. And then give him a dose of strychnine."

"Gee, Mr. Sampson."

They caught Mophead at last, halfway down toward the outer headland. Meg helped Joe while they led him home and locked him up in the backyard. Joe looked at him kindly. "You had no way of knowing that the meat wasn't meant for you. Especially with Charlie Chops messing about with it. You just thought it was a bit extra, didn't you?"

Meg laughed. "You'd better not say that to Stewy Sampson."

Mophead looked up with large eyes and wagged his tail halfheartedly. He still hadn't recovered from the terrifying feeling of the pronged fork in his rump.

"You're a good boy," Joe said.

Mophead, gazing up, suddenly burped. Nobody could have known that he had swallowed five big leg chops and eleven sausages before the table had collapsed.

"He's *not* a good boy," Meg said, "so don't tell him lies. If Stewy catches him at it again, he'll feed him to the sharks."

Joe turned away sadly. No matter what Mophead did, he always ended up in trouble.

4

Uncle Harry didn't try to get in touch with George Lane at once. He was too shrewd for that. Instead he telephoned the newspaper at Ceduna and asked the editor to print a story about Scarface—about the way he had gained his scar in the first place, about the way he had almost caught Joe, about the way he had sunk the tourists' boat, about his fearlessness, about his size and weight. It set people talking.

From there it soon went into the news bulletins of the local radio station, and then onto regional television. Before long it was in the national news of the big-city newspapers and Uncle Harry was being driven out of his mind by telephone calls from reporters and television cameramen all over the country. He had shown that he understood the strange hysteria of modern media that feeds on sensation. The story of a huge shark sinking a boat was sensational. The story of a boy being rescued in the nick of time was also sensational. Everybody wanted to know more about it. It was something for the headlines. It was big news.

Uncle Harry now played his master stroke. He telephoned George Lane in Adelaide and asked him if he would like to come to Cockle Bay to hunt Scarface. A good boat, the *Seahorse*, would be available. The local people thought that George should have the first option because he was the leading record holder. But if he was not interested they would get in touch with someone else.

George took the bait. "That monster is mine," he said at once. "Don't hire out your boat to anyone else. But I can't get over there until Easter. Can you hold off until then?"

"No problem," answered Uncle Harry. "We're delighted that you can come."

Uncle Harry was even more delighted than he was willing to say, because he knew that George Lane was a rich man who could pay his own expenses.

The newspapers and TV stations were ecstatic when they heard about it. George Lane appeared on all the television news programs discussing his catches and showing off his rods and reels. The radio stations arranged interviews with him, and the newspapers carried headlines such as HUNTING THE HUNTER and ST. GEORGE AND THE DRAGON.

Uncle Harry laughed at all the brouhaha. "St. George and the Dragon," he said. "What garbage."

"Oh I don't know," Meg answered. "Instead of riding a war-horse he'll be riding *Seahorse*, and instead of a long lance he'll have a fishing rod."

Her father scoffed. "We're talking about a *real* monster," he said, "not a paper one. A monster seventeen or twenty feet long with jaws like an excavator and teeth like knives. So let's not have any storybook nonsense. Scarface would make your fairytale dragons look like mermaids."

Meg smirked. "All the same, I hope Mr. Lane is a bit like a knight—tall and dark and brave."

As Easter drew near, the excitement in Cockle Bay increased. It was an unusual year because the public holiday for Anzac Day, commemorating the landing of Australian and New Zealand Army Corps at Gallipoli, fell on the Wednesday after Easter, so many people were taking a six-day break to go vacationing and camping along the coast. Some were staying near at hand so that they could inspect Scarface if George Lane should happen to bring him in.

Uncle Harry was tense. *Seahorse* had to be in first-class order. Spare fuel had to be loaded and ample supplies arranged. And there was the question of money. Although George Lane would be paying for the hire of the boat, Uncle Harry was letting him have it at such a cheap rate that it was doubtful whether he would break even. He would have to pay Herc Sampson full wages, especially since he was giving up his Easter holidays, and old Otto Minz would expect his usual fee for keeping the service station open and pumping gas.

Joe knew that his uncle was worried. He heard him talking about it at night to Aunt Ellen in their bedroom when everyone else was supposed to be asleep. Joe didn't intend to hear what they were saying. He wasn't an eavesdropper. But the house was so small and the walls were so thin that he couldn't help overhearing everything they said. That was how he was forewarned of some very startling news.

"We really must have a cook," Uncle Harry said. "An important fellow like George Lane will expect decent meals."

Joe heard Aunt Ellen sigh. "Yes, dear."

"But it's not only a question of finding one, especially over Easter. It's the cost."

"Yes dear."

"That's why I'm wondering about Meg and Joe."

Joe's stomach suddenly flopped and he sat bolt upright in bed. At the same time he heard Aunt Ellen give a shocked exclamation. "Oh, don't be ridiculous, Harry."

"It's not as stupid as it sounds."

"Of course it's stupid. Good heavens, they're only

children. I'm not going to have a daughter of mine—
or a nephew either, for that matter—poking about
out there with sharks and gaffs and flying fish hooks.
Not at their age."

"They could do it, Nell. I'm sure of it. And they'd
be safe."

"They're too young, Harry."

"All right, so they are, but they could do the job.
They could clean up the galley each day, make the
toast and coffee, fry a few eggs. And if we take
mainly simple stuff in the freezer—casseroles, stews,
pies—they could even heat up the main meals."

Aunt Ellen sighed again. "No, Harry."

"It would be good experience for them."

"They're still children."

"The two of them together would more than make
up for an adult."

"They're not strong enough."

"And it would save hundreds of dollars."

Joe, sitting up in bed with his eyes agog, could
scarcely contain himself. He wanted to leap out and
burst into their room shouting, "We can do it, we
can do it." Instead he had to live silently with his
secret, all night and all day. At school he had to
hug it to himself even when Nicky or Meg were
talking about Scarface and George Lane. Once or
twice when Meg looked at him sharply and said,
"Are you all right Joe? You're so quiet," he was on
the brink of telling her. But it was something he
wasn't supposed to know. Meg would think he'd

been spying on her father and mother. And the whole thing was still uncertain; it might fall through.

In the end Uncle Harry dropped the bombshell at the tea table about a week before Easter. He made it sound like a question, something he had only just thought of a moment earlier.

"How would you two like to work on *Seahorse* over the Easter break—as part of the crew?"

Meg almost gagged on her tea in ecstasy, and Joe did his best to sound surprised. As usual Maureen went into a tantrum when she realized she was going to be left behind, but her mother silenced her sternly.

Uncle Harry was beaming, not least because he had finally persuaded Aunt Ellen to accept the idea. "It's the chance of a lifetime," he said to Joe and Meg. "Some people would give their eyeteeth just to see a man like George Lane at work. But it won't be a pleasure cruise. You realize that?"

"Yes, Dad," Meg answered.

"We'll work like mad," Joe said.

"And you'll remember to keep out of the way, especially if they hook a shark," Aunt Ellen added darkly.

When he arrived a few days before Easter, George Lane was a disappointment. He was round faced, square shouldered, and bald. But he was as strong as a buffalo and he knew how to catch sharks.

For two days there was a flurry of preparation.

Seahorse had a big hatch cover that folded back to form a strong square platform. The hinged section was secured in place with two thick barrel bolts. The special swivel chair that George Lane had brought with him was fixed firmly in the center, and a low footrail was fastened in a circle near the outer perimeter. It was an ideal arrangement for big-game fishing.

"I like a low chair," George kept saying. "I like one that lets me haul until I'm nearly flat on my back. And I need one that spins as fast as a top," He swung the swivel from side to side. "And plenty of clear space all around—no stays, no stanchions, no obstacles. Just a nice low rail where I can brace my heels and get some traction."

He sat in the chair for the twentieth time, testing everything until he was satisfied that it was perfect. Then he went off to check his enormous assortment of fishing tackle: rods and reels, lines, traces, and hooks worth thousands of dollars.

After that they had to fit the crossarm near the stern for the lures, and a bracket for the oil drip. Mick Mareolas was sent off to catch four or five big stingrays and a few tuna for bait, and Uncle Harry loaded the stores.

Meanwhile Meg and Joe had packed and repacked their bags five times and had been given a crash course in cooking. Aunt Ellen despaired of Joe when it was his turn to fry bacon and eggs, because he let so many of the eggs slip off the griddle and finish up on the kitchen floor. However he did prove that he could boil water, heat stew, make coffee, and burn the toast.

Aunt Ellen also supervised the packing of such things as toothbrushes, combs, spare sweaters, and warm socks, and insisted that Meg should have her hair cut. She seemed to have a strange notion that long hair was certain to be caught in the propeller or the yardarm of George Lane's fishing reel. Normally Uncle Harry would have guffawed and told her she was a bigger fusspot than a mother duck, but he was too busy to notice.

There was a last-minute hitch over Herc Sampson, the main crewman and gaffer, who dislocated his knee a day before *Seahorse* was due to sail and came hopping along with a crutch to say that he couldn't make the trip. However his brother, Boxhead, was willing to fill the gap, and although he was not as strong as Herc, he had salt in his blood and he knew the ways of the sea.

On the Thursday before Easter, Meg and Joe raced home from school, seized their bags, and ran breathlessly down to the jetty. Aunt Ellen and Maureen walked down more slowly to wave good-bye. Half an hour later Boxhead slipped the moorings, and *Seahorse* headed gently down the channel toward the open sea. The great shark hunt had started.

5

The first task, of course, was to find Scarface. Although he hadn't been seen for some weeks, Uncle Harry was confident that he was still hanging about. "We'll find him," he said. "He likes cruising between Herringbone Shoal and Cockle Bay, and that's a small strip no more than four or five miles wide. We'll lay up under Seal Island tonight and put out a trail at first light."

George Lane sat on the deck, carefully checking his big reel. His bald head shone as if the evening breeze had just finished polishing it. "Find him for me," he said simply, "and I hope I'll be able to do the rest."

Meg, Joe, and Boxhead stood watching, trying to

figure out what kind of person he really was. Apart from the fact that he managed a business in the city and that he flew his own airplane, they didn't know much. Unlike many fisherman, he said very little. He never boasted, even though he held five fishing records. He never talked about the ones that sometimes got away, or even about the ones that didn't. He was more like a quiet gentleman from a library, or a book-lined study, than a fisherman. On the other hand they could see that he was a perfectionist; everything had to be just right. But that was understandable when he was preparing to do battle with a monster like Scarface. He could be risking his own life.

Uncle Harry brought *Seahorse* in under the lee of Seal Island and anchored for the night. Joe and Meg served the food—hot stew, thick slices of buttered bread, fruit and cream, and hot coffee—and then they did the dishes in the galley. By nine o'clock they were all in their bunks.

"Early start tomorrow, Joe," Uncle Harry said. "Five-o'clock breakfast."

Joe looked at Meg. "Whose turn?"

"Both of us."

"Okay."

Her father grinned. "I'll give you both a call."

Joe lay awake for a long time. All kinds of ideas crowded his mind. He liked the sea. He liked the gentle rocking of the boat, the sucking sound of the water against the hull, the feeling of space and peace all around. Perhaps he could work on a boat permanently. Perhaps he could even have a boat of his own someday and settle down in a place like Cockle Bay to make his own living in his own way. He'd like that. It would be better than going back to Melbourne, where there would be nothing but heartache and bad memories.

He dozed off at last, and within a minute or two— or so it seemed—Boxhead was shaking his bunk and yelling in his ear. "Wakey, wakey. Rise and shine. The sun'll be burning your eyes out in a minute." He eyed Joe. "Your partner's been up for twenty minutes."

Joe heaved himself up so suddenly that he bumped his head against the bracket above his bunk. "Meg has? Gosh, I've really slept late."

"D'you want to wash—or take a bath?" asked Boxhead. Joe sat rubbing his head and collecting his wits. He looked at Boxhead with a stupid expression on his face. He knew very well that there wasn't a bath on *Seahorse*; the little washroom was so narrow that you needed to be a stovepipe to turn around in it. But it was hard for Joe to think properly when his head was both fuzzy and painful at the same time.

"Bath?" he asked, befuddled.

"Overboard," answered Boxhead.

"Oh, a swim? Yes, I'd like that."

His uncle, who had been listening, put his head through the doorway. "Okay, just hold your horses for a second while I make sure the coast is clear."

Joe didn't understand. He was even more mystified when he heard the engine start momentarily and felt *Seahorse* swing on the mooring line. It lasted for no more than an instant before the engine cut out and everything was silent again. He struggled into his briefs.

"Okay," Uncle Harry called. "In you go. I'll get the rifle."

Joe's wits were still dull. "Rifle?"

"For the Charlie Arks. I'll stand guard." He saw the expression on Joe's face and laughed out loud. "Never jump overboard out here without taking precautions. Especially in the morning. Sharks like boats. They lie under them, motionless, dozing. They rub off their barnacles against the hull. If you jump in without looking, you could find yourself skylarking with a couple of pointers. They swim out from the shadow of the boat and join you. I've seen it happen."

"Holy mackerel," said Joe. He hesitated. "Maybe I'll just have a wash."

His uncle was still laughing. "You'll be okay. I started the engine and moved the boat to scare them off—just in case any were lurking underneath. But it's all clear. Anyway, I'll stand on deck with the .303. The water's like crystal—you could see a shark three hundred feet away."

Boxhead grabbed a towel and climbed up the stairway. "Come on," he yelled, "I'll beat you in."

They both ran along the deck in their briefs and leaped over the side with an enormous splash. The water was like a mirror. *Seahorse* stood up from it so motionlessly that she looked like a ship painted on canvas.

Joe was elated. "It's beautiful."

"Flat calm," answered Boxhead, pushing the hair from his eyes. "You don't often see it like this out here."

Just then Meg came running along the deck and dived in as neatly as a professional. "Look at that," Boxhead cried. "She's practicing for the Olympics."

Joe had never swum in such a sea. He had never felt such joy. It was almost as if his body didn't belong to him, it felt so light and clean and swift. He and Meg and Boxhead dived and rolled under the water like seals, their bodies gliding fast and free. Then they shot up and broke the surface so swiftly that the water fell from their shining shoulders in a shower. They could see the clean sandy bottom below them, scattered with bits of weed and shell, and the cable sloping down from the bow to the anchor in the distance. The world was all water and soft translucent light. And life was the marvelous movement of their bodies.

"Okay," yelled Uncle Harry when they surfaced for the tenth time. "All aboard."

"Coming."

They clambered back on board and stood toweling themselves briskly.

"Best swim I ever had," Joe said, panting and rubbing.

"Me too," Meg answered. "It was like swimming in light. I felt like a seal."

"You looked like a mermaid, only your hair's too short."

"All right, all right," said Uncle Harry. "Down to the galley; there's work to do."

A minute later Meg was standing at the stove frying bacon and eggs and Joe was making toast and coffee. Boxhead flipped up the little collapsible table in the cabin so that the five of them could eat in a civilized way. George Lane sat quietly at one end, sipping his coffee and staring out the porthole.

"Well, what do you think?" Boxhead asked. "Is today the big day?"

George shook his head. "Too flat."

Uncle Harry agreed. "Sharks like broken water. They get fidgety in a dead calm." He heaved himself up and padded onto the deck. "Still, we'll give it a try. We can't just sit around all day."

They laid the first trail along the edge of the reef. George Lane knelt near the stern, adjusting the drip on the whale-oil can. He had trouble getting it right; at first it was too fast, then too slow. However, in the end he seemed to be satisfied and sat watching the oily slick streaming out behind them. As the drops of oil hit the water, they spread out into a narrow lane. It was like a beacon. They knew that any sharks swimming across it would turn and follow it up toward the boat. Whale oil was something they couldn't resist. And when they reached the boat, the lures would be there, waiting and beckoning—big chunks of stingray and tuna hanging from the crossarm just above the water.

But today *Seahorse* was out of luck. The sharks seemed to have disappeared. "All gone for a stroll," Uncle Harry said sourly. "On a normal day they're as thick as weeds out here."

After lunch they laid down another trail a few miles nearer to the coast, and finally a cross trail at right angles to the other two between Cockle Bay and the reef. But still they saw nothing.

"Too calm," George Lane repeated. "We need a little wind."

Uncle Harry was taking regular radio calls and checking the barometer. "It should be better in a day or two. There's some weather coming in from the Bight. That'll chop things up."

The forecaster was right. On Saturday the wind shifted to the southwest and blew hard for most of the day. *Seahorse* had to creep in close under the leeward shore of Seal Island for shelter. By Sunday things had improved, but there were still whitecaps on the sea, and the fangs of the reef were snarling and slavering.

After breakfast Uncle Harry went up on deck and stood gazing all around. He looked at George Lane questioningly. "Too rough?"

"It'll settle. By lunchtime it should be just right."

They spent the morning getting everything ship-shape. Meg and Joe cleaned the galley and Boxhead swabbed the deck. George Lane took some big slabs of stingray and tuna from the freezer and spent a long time preparing the lures so that they were left hanging at just the right height above the water. Then he checked his rods and reels for the twentieth time.

Just before midday Uncle Harry started the main engine, and *Seahorse* nudged her way out into the open water. It was still a bit rough, but he knew every square yard of the sea in these parts, and so he was able to hold a course down the sheltered side of the reef. George Lane opened the tap on the whale-oil can and set it at a very fast drip.

When they had laid a trail for a mile or two, Uncle Harry swung the boat around in a circle near a rocky outcrop of the reef and slowed down to a crawl. "Mermaid Rock," he called. "It's a good spot. Usually crawling with sharks."

He had barely finished speaking when Boxhead gave a great shout. "Look, look. Here they come."

Uncle Harry cut the engine altogether and *Seahorse* wallowed silently for a moment in the swell. The breeze and the tide took her away from the reef, so there was no danger.

Three sharks were flashing around the boat. They were obviously excited, stirred up by the whale oil and the lures. Most of the time they were swift flitting shadows just below the surface, but now and then one of their dorsal fins cut the water like a big triangular knife.

George Lane was standing tensely by the starboard rail, peering hard. "Small fellows," he called to Boxhead.

"How big d'you reckon?"

"Ten feet. Eleven hundred pounds, maybe."

"I guess it's a start."

"Sure."

"You going to give 'em a go?"

"Not if something bigger turns up."

They waited patiently while several more sharks arrived, but they were not big. Of the six or seven now swimming about in a frenzy, the heaviest probably weighed no more than thirteen hundred pounds. But it was fast and aggressive. Without warning it swam in from the stern and reared up at one of the starboard lures, tearing off a big chunk before crashing back into the water. Then it circled wide as if preparing for another run.

George Lane watched it carefully. "This guy could be worth a try," he said, "if I use my lightest line."

"Why not?" Uncle Harry said. "You'll be ready for Scarface then."

"It'll toughen up your shoulders," Boxhead added.

George Lane seemed to make up his mind. "Okay," he said. "Let's try."

Uncle Harry sprang forward, calling to Boxhead. "Right. Lures up, decks clear."

George Lane buckled on his harness and set himself squarely in the chair with his feet braced against the traction rail at the edge of the platform. Boxhead baited the big shark hook with a special lump of tuna and stood poised, grasping the stainless steel trace a yard or so above the bait.

"He'll come around to starboard again," George Lane called, "to the same spot where he took the lure. They always do."

He was right. Within a minute or two the shark was back, angling in toward the very spot where the lure had been hanging. Boxhead leaned forward and virtually hung out the bait in place of the lure. The shark came with a rush, opening its jaws and wolfing the bait, hook and all.

Uncle Harry jumped back into the wheelhouse, calling to Meg and Joe as he did so. "Stay clear now; give George room to move."

Boxhead retreated too, crouching near the rail on the port side, waiting watchfully in case of emergencies.

Joe and Meg were astonished. They had never seen a big-game fisherman at work. Strangely, for the first few seconds there was no action at all. The shark seemed to be lolling near the surface, quite unconcerned.

"What's happening?" Meg asked in a whisper.

Her father chuckled. "The shark doesn't even know it's hooked. George hasn't struck yet. He's waiting for it to take the bait good and proper." But as he spoke the shark suddenly felt the pull of the line. George Lane jerked the rod to embed the hook as deeply as he could, and the next instant the line started racing off the reel like a high-speed spool in a clothing factory. The shark ran straight out from the stern of the boat. Within moments it was three hundred feet out, then six hundred, then almost a thousand.

"Back up," yelled George Lane. "I've only got two thousand feet of line."

Uncle Harry threw the engine into reverse, easing *Seahorse* back gently at half speed astern. As soon as he had gained a little slack, George reeled in desperately, trying to keep the line taut. When his quarry veered, he swung his chair so that it always faced the direction of the shark's travel. The big fish kept well below the surface, plunging down into deep water. There was nothing spectacular about the battle, no sensational scenes like films of tuna seemingly dancing on their tails or giant marlin leaping into the air and crashing back in monstrous fountains of spray. This was a grim, silent struggle with an unseen adversary.

Yet George Lane seemed to know exactly what was going on. He had an uncanny knack of following the shark's movements, as if the thin line that joined them together kept on transmitting secret messages up through his hands. He swung and veered and straightened up, constantly changing direction. Once he even unbuckled his harness frantically and ran along *Seahorse*'s sides as the shark doubled back like lightning and swam right underneath the boat. But a few seconds later he was back in the chair, heaving on the rod and reeling quickly, heaving again and reeling, without a pause in the struggle.

Beads of perspiration began to stand out on his face and little trickles ran down his forehead toward his eyes. He called to Boxhead to wipe them away. When the shark made one of its runs, the reel raced and the line streamed away again like a belt from a flywheel. There was no point in trying to stop it. A line with a breaking strain of a few pounds couldn't be jerked hastily when a thirteen-hundred-pound weight was threshing about on the other end of it. It was likely to snap like cotton thread. As far as Joe was concerned it even *looked* like cotton thread.

Thirty minutes went by, sixty minutes, ninety minutes. George Lane's face was as red and moist as a piece of freshly cooked corned beef. His bald head shone in the afternoon sun, his shirt was wet with perspiration. But at last the shark began to tire and the line began to creep back onto the reel, inch by inch—a thousand feet of it, thirteen hundred feet. George put on more brake, forcing the big fish to pull even harder. Seventeen hundred feet.

"Get ready," he called to Boxhead. "Gaffs out?"

"Okay," answered Boxhead excitedly.

"Grab the steel trace when it comes up to the head of the rod. But be careful. Pull firmly and evenly so that he comes up alongside the boat steadily—a nice easy motion." George was gasping out his instructions like an exhausted athlete. "If you pause or pull unevenly, he'll roll and run. Then we'll have to go through it all over again."

Joe and Meg were on pins and needles. They caught glimpses of the shark now, swimming under the surface in a stunned sort of way.

"Here comes the trace," George Lane called.

The stainless steel wire glinted in the sunlight as it came up out of water. It was enormously strong, with a breaking strain of almost a ton. Under game-fishing rules it could be used to hold the hook so that the great teeth of the shark couldn't cut or fray the line.

There was a splash near the stern of the boat as the shark broke the surface. "Here he comes. Careful now."

Boxhead reached out, seized the trace, and began to pull the shark firmly forward until it lay alongside.

George Lane unbuckled himself and leaped from the platform. "Look out he doesn't roll."

Boxhead was nervous. "What if he does?"

"Let him go. Then I'll have to reel him in again." He watched Boxhead sharply. "And for heaven's sake don't coil the trace on the deck. Drop it down between the shark and the boat. If a bit winds around your leg and the shark suddenly dives, you'll either have your leg torn off or you'll be towed about under the water until you're dead."

Luckily all went well. A few minutes later the shark was safely gaffed and lashed to the side of the boat. The battle was over. It had lasted exactly two hours.

"What now?" Meg asked. She was strangely quiet. Perhaps she had as much sympathy for the shark as she did for the fisherman.

"Might as well weigh him," her father said.

George nodded. "I'd like to know, even if he's not a record."

They towed the shark back to Cockle Bay and hoisted it up on the gantry at the end of the jetty. Aunt Ellen and Maureen came running down, and a small crowd gathered quickly to watch the sight. Heads craned forward to read the figures on the scales.

Charlie Chops was the weighing master, and he put on his most official voice. "Please stand back; stand back please."

"Watch what you're doing," Mick Mareolas called rudely. "And don't give us short weight, the way you usually do."

There were guffaws of laughter all around. Charlie ignored them as he scrutinized the scales. "Thirteen hundred and sixty pounds," he yelled. Some people clapped and a few shook George Lane's hand. But Porker Bacon was rude. "You're supposed to catch Scarface," he said, "not a baby. You could take this thing out of Scarface's rib and he wouldn't notice the difference."

"We're going back now," Uncle Harry answered curtly. "You tell us where Scarface is and George'll bring him in, all right."

They took on some extra supplies and sailed out to sea again in the late afternoon. By sunset they were back at their favorite mooring place near Seal Island.

6

It was a fine night, with a cool breeze from the south. "Good shark weather," Boxhead said. "We'll get Scarface this time, for sure."

George Lane smiled. "It's a bit like a lottery, you know—finding one particular shark in the whole wide sea."

"Like tracking down a flea on an elephant," Uncle Harry grunted.

George nodded. "And even if we find him, we still have to catch him."

"You'll do that all right."

George scoffed. "I've lost more big sharks than I've caught."

Joe was disappointed. "Why? Do they break the line?"

"Anything can happen. They snap the line, run over a reef with it, snag it on rocks, roll up in the trace." He paused as if remembering all the disasters of the past. "The clutch on the reel can get red-hot and jam, the teeth can shear off, the rod can break. A shark that weighs a ton can snap the hook or straighten it out. It can throw up the bait or charge the boat and wind the line around the propeller."

Joe and Meg listened in awe. They hoped that the hunt for Scarface would go on for weeks and months so that they could sit on deck urging George Lane to tell them the thrilling stories about the fish he had caught—and the ones that had got away. But Meg's father kept his eye on them and bundled them off to bed with promises of hard work and high excitement in the morning.

He was right. On Monday morning they had sharks following the boat like hyenas—small ones that flitted about greedily and inquisitively, medium-sized fellows that rushed fearlessly at the lures, and two or three big ones more than thirteen feet long that cruised slyly in the shadowy waters beyond the boat. But there was still no sign of Scarface.

In the end George Lane decided to try for one of the big ones on a tiny line in the hope of breaking a record. But he had no luck. Although he managed to hook the biggest one, after a lot of frustration, he held it for less than ten minutes. For the shark cleverly rolled over and over in the trace until it reached the line. Then its harsh hide, rougher than sandpaper, sawed through the thread in an instant.

"Oh blast," shouted Uncle Harry from the wheel-house.

"Bad luck," said Boxhead, more disappointed than George Lane himself.

George reeled in the slack line without a word. Then he went to get a new trace and hook. "It happens," he said quietly. "You win some and you lose some."

They chased about on the ocean for two more days. Sharks followed the boat, sharks worked themselves into a frenzy over the slicks of whale oil, sharks lunged at the lures. But there was no sign of Scarface. Joe and Meg were close to despair; even Uncle Harry was getting edgy and impatient. Only George Lane remained calm. Nothing seemed to upset him. Perhaps that was why he was such a great fisherman.

"You have to learn to be patient," he said quietly. "Sometimes you have to wait for years for the really big one. And sometimes he gets away even then."

On Tuesday evening *Seahorse* lay in the lee of Seal Island again. Before going to bed, Uncle Harry stomped up on deck with some bait. "We'll put out a bit of chum," he announced. "And we'll let the lures hang there all night."

The sea air and the hard work seemed to suit Meg, but they made Joe sleepy. He had grown so used to the gentle rocking of the boat that he slept like a log at night, and Boxhead had to shake him in the morning.

But even Joe couldn't sleep through the commotion that broke out in the early-morning darkness on Wednesday. He was suddenly aware of a violent thump, and then *Seahorse* tilted sharply to starboard before swinging back again and rocking from side to side. All her timbers creaked. A few moments later there was a terrible grinding sound at the stern, and then the whole boat pointed her bow upward and began plunging up and down.

Voices and cries broke out all around. Uncle Harry was out of his bunk in a flash, bounding up on deck with a flashlight in his hand. His short pajama pants sagged so far below his waist that they were on the point of falling down altogether. Boxhead, George Lane, and Meg were close behind him.

"A big fellow," yelled Uncle Harry even before he had seen anything at all. "He's got the prop in his jaws."

For the second time in a week Joe almost brained himself by leaping up too violently from his bunk. He reeled back, trying to get his bearings. By the time he had staggered out and followed the others, Uncle Harry was already down near the stern, flicking the beam of the flashlight, stabbing it about like a white blade in the darkness. Meg was on the port side, Boxhead and George Lane on the starboard. Joe hurried down and stood beside Meg. "See anything?" he asked excitedly.

As if in answer to the question, a huge shark suddenly reared up at Meg's side, lunging at one of the lures. Her father's flashlight swung onto it, and for a second Meg and Joe found themselves looking down into the cavernous mouth of the monster. The vast jaws were wide open, and the torch glinted momentarily on the circle of fearful triangular teeth, each edge more than two inches long. Shocked beyond belief, they had a fleeting image of prehistoric knives—knives that tore and mutilated flesh more than they cut it. Then the gigantic fish fell back with a splash like a tidal wave. The jaws snapped shut, and there in the beam of the flashlight, as clear as a drawn line, was a great scar from the left eye to the edge of the upper jaw.

"It's *him*," cried Meg. "It's him. It's Scarface!"

Her father was breathing heavily as he darted from side to side, trying to follow the movement of the shark with the beam of the flashlight. But it was impossible. Scarface slipped away into the shadows and disappeared. "It was him, all right," he cried. "There's no other shark quite like him."

For once George Lane seemed excited. "Just stay around," he said in a hushed voice. "Please, Scarface, just hang around until daylight. Go for the lures as often as you like."

"It's a good sign," Uncle Harry said. "He's hungry."

George looked at his watch. "Four o'clock. We have to keep him here for two more hours."

"There's nothing we can do about it now—except hope."

Boxhead was almost naked. He had goose bumps on his arms and legs and his shoulders were shivering. "I'm frozen," he said. "I'm going back to bed."

They all followed him below and crawled gratefully into their bunks, but nobody slept a wink. They were too tense, listening for sounds and movements beyond the hull.

"There he is again," Uncle Harry said suddenly. They heard it only too clearly—a long rasping sound like sandpaper being dragged along the timbers outside. "Probably scratching his barnacles."

Once there was a metallic rattle near the bow, and the boat rocked strongly for a second or two.

"What's that?" Joe asked in alarm.

"He's got the anchor chain in his teeth," Uncle Harry answered. "He's shaking it—like a dog with a bone."

"I had no idea," Joe said, trying to hide the uneasiness in his voice, "that they could be so vicious with boats."

His uncle laughed in the darkness. "They'll do anything—bite chunks out of the stern, leave teeth stuck in the transom, rattle the anchor chain, try to chew up the propeller, smash off the lure arm. You name it, they'll do it."

"It's a good sign," George Lane said quietly. "The more aggressive he is, the better the chance that he'll take the baits."

"Has anybody stopped to think," Meg said nervously, "that the only thing separating us from him at the moment is an inch or two of timber?"

"Yes," answered Joe, "he's right next to your left elbow. He can smell your blood."

She snorted. "He can probably smell your socks, Joe. They're enough to turn on any shark in the sea."

When the first light of dawn finally silvered the portholes, they all hurried up on deck. There was no sign of Scarface. "Blast," said Boxhead. "I thought we had him this time."

"He's old and shrewd," George Lane said. "He's going to give us a run for our money."

At breakfast they had a short council of war. "Scarface can't be far from here," Uncle Harry said. "It's less than an hour since he was messing around with the boat, so he can't have swum very far."

"And sharks don't swim in a straight line," George added. "They hang around and double back and poke their noses into this and that."

"So we'll lay down the whale oil in a circle this time," Uncle Harry said, "instead of in a straight line."

Boxhead was impressed. "That's a good idea. Then we'll just hang in the slick and wait for him to follow it around."

Meg was skeptical. "What if Scarface is already outside the circle?"

"We'll make it big enough to prevent that," her father said firmly.

They didn't have to carry out their plan. Less than half a mile from the island, when *Seahorse* was just beginning to make her turn with fresh lures beckoning and the whale-oil dripping, Boxhead gave a great shout. "He's back! He's back!"

It was exactly eight o'clock. Joe had finished washing the breakfast dishes and Meg was cleaning the stove in the galley. They stumbled up on deck in time to see George Lane buckling himself jubilantly into his harness and Boxhead leaning over toward the port-side lures. Three or four smaller sharks were swimming about energetically, darting this way and that.

"Nuisances," said Uncle Harry impatiently. "They'll mess things up if we're not careful."

George Lane tightened a buckle and looked up. "Are you sure the big fellow is Scarface?"

"Certain of it," answered Meg and Boxhead together. Boxhead pointed. "Look, you can see the trademark on his snout as clear as daylight."

The huge shark had ripped away part of the inside port lure and was coming around in a wide circle for more.

"Up," yelled Uncle Harry tensely to Boxhead. "Get that lure up. I want to offer him the bait instead." Everyone watched breathlessly. "You ready, George?" he asked, without looking over his shoulder.

"Ready." George seemed as calm as a judge.

"Here we go then."

Just as the huge fish came back to the spot where the lure had been hanging, Uncle Harry deftly lowered the bait in its place. But instead of opening its vast jaws and swallowing it, the shark veered suddenly and circled away.

"Blast. He's a sharp old monster."

"The big ones always are. They've learned too much."

"I'll try again."

They made five more attempts and had five more failures. Uncle Harry was red with frustration. "I don't think he's going to take the bait," he called. "He'll get tired of this soon and swim away. Then we'll lose him for good."

"Try throwing it farther out," George Lane said. "Tow it in front of him with the trace."

The trick worked. As Scarface came around for the sixth time, the big bait of tuna and stingray appeared to be moving away from him like a living creature. The great shark swept forward, opened its jaws, and swallowed.

"Got him," Uncle Harry said fiercely.

"Wait." George Lane didn't strike at once. He

paused for a few seconds while the shark continued its forward movement. Then, just as it felt the evil touch of the steel wire, George whipped up the rod and embedded the hook firmly.

"He's hooked," yelled Boxhead. "You've got him."

"Not yet," hissed George. "Not by a long shot."

Now Scarface ran. The line whipped out like a bolt from a harpoon gun. Although George had put three thousand feet of the best quality line onto his reel, it wasn't long before he was shouting, "Back up, back up," to Uncle Harry in the wheelhouse. It had to be done quickly and efficiently. One mistake, one slight jolt, one moment's delay while the reel was still screaming, and Scarface would snap the line and go free.

George Lane concentrated with every nerve. While the shark was moving at full power, he didn't even attempt to reel in the line. It was up to Uncle Harry to keep *Seahorse* skillfully in the right position. For the moment the skipper was just as important as the fisherman. Joe wondered what would have happened if they had fastened themselves to Scarface with a rope instead of a fishing line; perhaps he would have towed the boat all over the Antarctic Ocean.

Suddenly George Lane swiveled in his chair and started reeling desperately. At the same time he yelled, "Forward! Forward! He's running this way."

Scarface was a wily creature. Within seconds he had raced right underneath the boat and run out to sea on the starboard side. If it hadn't been for George Lane's skill and experience, the line would have been snagged and broken before any of them could have blinked an eye. As it was, George leaped out of his chair, swung the rod far out over the stern to allow the line to pass freely underneath, and then sprang back to his seat again, clipping the catches on his harness before Joe had quite realized what had happened.

"Slow down, slow down," George shouted to Uncle Harry, sensing yet another maneuver on the part of the shark. "He's going deep. When he comes up he'll be going like a rocket."

And so the battle of wits went on. George played Scarface very carefully, sometimes reeling, sometimes letting the line run. Then for the first time he increased the drag on the reel and pressed his gloved hand against it to increase the braking action. Scarface responded spectacularly. He raced upward and away, breaking the surface suddenly like a colossal marlin. For a second he seemed to be held there—a two-ton monster momentarily airborne—and then fell back into the sea in a roaring plume of white water and spray.

"Look at *that*," cried Meg, goggle-eyed.

"Moses," said Boxhead.

Uncle Harry was incredulous. "In thirty years I've never seen anything like that."

"Neither have I," said George Lane, straining on his rod.

"Normally sharks don't do that, surely?"

"This is not a normal shark."

Scarface ran straight out to sea again, whipping the line off the reel. It spun like a top.

"Back up, back up again," yelled George Lane once more. "He's really got a flea in his ear this time."

The struggle went on and on. George put more drag on the line, as much as he dared, but he had to be very careful not to overdo it. He knew how easy it was to break the line.

Perspiration streamed from his cheeks and forehead. Every few minutes he asked Meg or Joe to wipe his face with a damp cloth to prevent the perspiration from getting into his eyes. "It smarts like mad," he said. "Must be the salt. I had no idea I was so salty."

Joe and Meg soon found themselves involved in George's battle just as fully as Uncle Harry and Boxhead were. They became George's attendants, fetching a new glove, a headband, a handkerchief. Every twenty minutes one of them brought up a glass of cold water and held it carefully while George slurped quickly and greedily. They had to be prepared to leap out of the way instantly if the shark changed direction or swung erratically. Joe was keyed up as he had never been before. It was more than excitement. It was responsibility. And it was danger. He was part of a team, and together they were going to catch the biggest shark in the world. People would talk about it for years.

Meg, on the other hand, was hesitant about the whole thing. She understood the argument in favor of catching Scarface, but she seemed to feel sorry for him at the same time.

By twelve o'clock George Lane began to gain ground. By half past twelve he had reeled in all but three hundred feet of line, and by one o'clock they could see the steel trace coming in toward the boat.

"By Jove, you'll do it yet," cried Uncle Harry. "I think you've got him beat."

He spoke too soon. Suddenly Scarface turned and ran, and the line raced off the reel again—three hundred feet, five hundred, seven hundred.

"Oh no." Joe sounded as if he wanted to cry. George Lane said nothing. He just grimaced, and as soon as the shark's run had ended, he started the backbreaking task of reeling in the line once more, inch by inch, foot by foot.

Twenty minutes later he had almost regained all the ground he had lost. The trace was again visible in the water, moving surely and steadily toward the stern of the boat and the nodding rod above it.

"Ready back there?" George Lane called, without taking his eyes off the line. "Who's going to take the trace?"

Uncle Harry looked quickly at Boxhead. "D'you think you can handle him?"

Boxhead hesitated. "Maybe you'd better take him, Mr. Blake. You know more about it than I do."

Uncle Harry was down in a flash. "Okay, you man the wheelhouse."

Joe knew how Boxhead felt. It was better that a grown man should take the risk.

"Cut the motor," Uncle Harry called. "We'll drift from here on."

He glanced at Meg and Joe. "Better stand well back. This is dangerous work."

"Here comes the trace," George Lane gasped. "Take it easy, Harry. He could be faking." George wound the reel grimly. He seemed to be grinding his teeth as he did it. The steel trace left the water and started to rise up toward the rod. Uncle Harry leaned over, his arm ready.

"Easy now, easy." In spite of his exhaustion, George Lane was still intensely alert.

"Just a bit more," Uncle Harry called.

"Right. Take it firmly and smoothly."

Uncle Harry leaned over farther still. Then, with a quick grasp, he seized the steel wire and began hauling it forward, dropping the surplus length of trace down beside the hull as he moved carefully along the starboard side. At the same time the great shark broke the surface near the stern and seemed to hover there for a moment like a kraken that had just emerged from the deep.

"Look at the size of him," Boxhead said in awe.

Joe stared unbelievingly. "Moses," he said to Meg.

"And to think we were swimming in the bay with him." Joe could never forget the day he had been rescued at the jetty with a second to spare.

Meg's father, every muscle tense, was concentrating totally on the line as he drew the monster slowly up beside the boat. "You've got a world record here, George," he said quietly. "He would have to weigh four thousand pounds."

"Maybe," George answered.

"He's *enormous*. He's twenty feet long and I reckon he's thirteen feet around the girth."

Scarface was almost beside the boat now, partly below and partly above the surface. Little ripples broke over him like waves over a half-submerged rock.

"Right, give me the big gaff," Uncle Harry said to Boxhead. "Gently, gently."

But just as Boxhead was about to pass the handle over to him, Meg yelled a warning. "Look out! He's rolling."

"Blast."

"He's diving."

Uncle Harry tried desperately to hold on to the trace, but it was hopeless. Scarface moved forward and downward like a juggernaut. There was no checking him. The wire was wrenched from Uncle Harry's hand, cutting and burning the flesh as it went.

"Let him go, let him go," cried George Lane. "I'll have to reel him back."

The line ran out once more, and George swiveled urgently in the chair to keep his rod at the right angle. Uncle Harry flexed his hand, opening and shutting it painfully, staring at the bloodstained palm. "A close call," he said grimly. "We nearly had him."

George Lane heaved on the rod and started reeling. "You've never really got 'em," he said philosophically, "until you've really got 'em."

And so the battle started all over again. George Lane looked completely bushed, but he didn't let up for an instant. His face was flushed and spongy, and his shirt wringing wet with perspiration, but his big shoulders heaved at the rod as strongly as ever and his hand cranked the reel steadily. Half an hour later he had the steel trace out of the water again, glinting momentarily in the sun.

"I'll take it a bit quicker," Uncle Harry said as he reached out for the wire a second time. "I think I was too slow before."

But he didn't get an opportunity. No sooner had he seized the wire than the great shark, as if sensing a trap, suddenly threshed like a whale and swam away ponderously. Its pull was irresistible. Again Uncle Harry had the steel wrenched from his grasp, and again it cut the flesh in the palm of his hand.

"Devil fish," he yelled angrily. "Why can't you learn when you're beaten?"

"He's not beaten yet," George Lane panted. "Not by a long shot."

Joe looked anxiously at his watch. It was almost two o'clock, way past lunchtime. George had been battling Scarface for six hours. Surely it couldn't go on much longer.

"Third time lucky," Uncle Harry said as George Lane started reeling in the huge shark yet again. "If we don't get him this time, we ought to give up."

"Don't say that," George wheezed. "Not after all the sweat I've lost."

"Have you ever had to reel in a fish more than three times?" Meg asked.

"No, but I've never hooked a fish like this one before."

As the trace came up for the third time, Uncle Harry seized it and hauled forward quickly. It was a mistake. He accidentally jerked the line, and Scarface reacted violently. He rolled, threshed, and dived steeply. Uncle Harry tried to hang on to prevent the run, thinking he could hold an exhausted shark if he hauled hard enough. There was no danger of the trace snapping, because it had a breaking strain of a ton. But it was a silly thing to do. Uncle Harry was almost pulled overboard before he finally let go, and his hand was cut badly again. It was becoming a bloodstained mess.

George Lane started reeling Scarface in for the fourth time. He grimaced when Uncle Harry apologized. "Maybe next time," he said.

But it wasn't to be next time, or the time after

that. The unbelievable battle went on and on. Six times George Lane hauled the great shark up to the boat, and six times it broke away again before it could be gaffed. By three o'clock in the afternoon George Lane gasped out that his backbone was pulp and his arms felt like mashed potatoes. Uncle Harry's hand was so bad that he couldn't close it properly to grip the trace.

Boxhead was worried. "Your hand is finished," he called. "Let me try next time."

George Lane looked at Uncle Harry and nodded. "Let him. You'd better put something on that hand and bandage it up."

And so it came about that Boxhead seized the trace when Scarface came up to the boat for the seventh time. He seemed to be doing well. He moved forward smoothly, keeping his eyes fixed on the shark, calling for Uncle Harry to be ready with the gaffs. So intently was he concentrating that he didn't even notice the surplus trace at his feet. Instead of drooping down into the water between the shark and the boat, it had accidentally fallen across the stern, looped under one corner of the platform, and trailed around the stanchions at the edge of the deck.

Even George Lane failed to see it. He was so exhausted that he could barely lift his head.

"Keep him coming," Uncle Harry said quietly. "You're doing fine."

But just as he lifted the gaff and moved forward,

the great fish rolled and dived for the seventh time.

"Let go," yelled Uncle Harry. "Let go. Let go." Then his cry suddenly changed into a desperate shout of danger. "Look out. The trace. The trace."

Joe and Meg saw it at the same moment and yelled too, but all their warnings were too late. As the shark plunged away, the steel wire snagged firmly on the stanchions and coiled itself around the corner of the platform. There was a grinding noise, followed by the terrible sound of splintering wood. Joe gaped as the bolts holding down the platform were torn out through the timber like tacks through cardboard. At the same time there was a sharp crack, almost like a rifle shot, as the steel snapped. Beyond the boat the water swirled in a brief flurry, and then there was silence.

Scarface was free.

7

What a woebegone group the crew of *Seahorse* were as they sailed back to Cockle Bay that evening! To add to their misery, the weather turned foul with a cold wind from the south, all teeth and sharp edges.

Uncle Harry stood in the wheelhouse with one hand wrapped in a bloodstained bandage, staring at the rising whitecaps. George Lane sat limply in the stern with his arms on his knees and his body bent like a hunchback's. Meg and Joe worked in the galley listlessly, saying nothing, and poor Boxhead went from place to place in an agony of self-condemnation.

"Gosh I'm sorry, Mr. Lane," he said over and over. "It was all my fault."

George Lane moved one hand in a tired gesture. "It happens," he answered tonelessly.

"I didn't see the trace. Honest, I didn't even see it."

"It was an accident."

"But it was my fault. You wouldn't have lost him otherwise."

"We could have lost him in a hundred ways."

Uncle Harry overheard them and shouted from the wheelhouse. "At least you've got a story to tell about the one that got away. Nearly eight hours of battling, and you brought him up to the boat seven times. Nobody can ever match a story like that."

George Lane smiled wanly. "I guess that's better than nothing."

"If it hadn't been for me, you would have landed him," Boxhead wailed. "We'd be taking him in to the gantry now."

George got up stiffly. "The gantry wouldn't have held him, and the scales would never have weighed him."

"Yes, you missed a new world record," Uncle Harry called. "It would never have been beaten." He eyed George silently. "Disappointed?"

"I suppose. Everyone likes breaking a record."

Meg and Joe came up just then carrying mugs of hot coffee. Meg handed one to George. "Are you going to try again, Mr. Lane?"

He smiled openly for the first time since Scarface had escaped. "Not today."

"Sometime?"

"Maybe, if Scarface is still about. I'll have to talk it over with your dad."

As they came up the channel toward the sheltered water of the bay, Joe stood looking out at the headlands and the dunes and the houses of the little town. The place was starting to feel like home. He took a deep breath. He was aware at once of a dozen smells that he had never known before coming to Cockle Bay—salty smells, damp seaweedy smells, sandy seashore smells. The spray had stopped whipping off the bows, but the deck was still wet, the ropes and handrails dripping. Tomorrow the sun would dry them out, leaving glittering crystals of salt here and there like tiny diamonds, pinhead points of light. Tomorrow? Tomorrow their battle with Scarface would be history. Tomorrow school would start again. Tomorrow he would have to look ahead instead of back.

"What are you thinking about, Joe?" George Lane asked. "A nice warm bed?"

Joe turned and smiled. "No, I was thinking about Cockle Bay—and what happens next."

For a day or two nobody seemed to know what was likely to happen next. The people of the town were astonished at the George Lane story, and disappointed that it had ended in failure. They wanted to know more. Boxhead went about the town with a hangdog expression, trying to avoid their questions, and Uncle Harry grew sick and tired of people who wanted to see his hand. The happiest inhabitant of Cockle Bay was Mophead, who greeted Joe's return with a wild dance that took several hours to complete.

Meg and Joe, of course, were stars in the school yard, and they had to repeat their story over and over again. They were even invited by the principal to describe their exploits to an assembly of the whole school. Nicky gazed at Meg adoringly while she was speaking, convinced that she was the most beautiful heroine in the world. Both Joe and Meg realized that they would have to sail in *Seahorse* again to keep up their reputations.

In the meantime George Lane had to go back to Adelaide to attend to important business there, but he was anxious to return to Cockle Bay in a few weeks for one last battle with Scarface—unless, of course, the great shark had decided to leave the place forever.

Uncle Harry had a long talk with George Lane before he left. After that he had long talks with Stewy Sampson and some of the other fishermen, and last of all he had a very short talk with Mr. Harding, who had come up from Port Lincoln again to pester him about money. This time he was more unpleasant than ever. If a sum of three thousand dollars were not paid by the middle of May, he said, he would see that Uncle Harry was declared bankrupt and arrange to seize his possessions. That was his last word. There would be no more warnings.

Aunt Ellen was very upset. Joe came upon her unexpectedly in the kitchen the next day, standing red-eyed by the sink, and although she tried to cover it up, Joe knew she had been crying. It made him just as upset as she was. And when Meg came in shortly afterward she also guessed the truth and was as miserable as the rest of them. Even Maureen sensed that something was wrong.

The weather turned tearful too. Great cloud banks rolled in from the sea and lowered over the coast, wrapping the town in gloom. Rain fell steadily, unceasingly, for two whole days. It was something so unusual that poor Charlie Chops bogged his truck in front of his own shop. But the farmers were jubilant, because at last the long drought had broken and they could hope for a good season, for a change.

It was also a blessing for Uncle Harry, because suddenly the price of sheep went up dramatically. Farmers wanted to restock their flocks, even if they had to borrow money from the banks to do it. There was a severe shortage of animals.

"Herbie Driver has offered to buy our sheep," Joe heard Uncle Harry say to Aunt Ellen one night when they were all in bed. "He knows we need the money."

Aunt Ellen was bitter. "Bad news always travels fast."

"They all want to stock up."

"What did you say?"

"I said we'd think about it."

Joe pulled the covers up to his ears. Once again he was overhearing the conversations of grown-ups, and once again he felt guilty about it.

"I thought we might offer him a hundred lambing ewes if he's willing to pay thirty dollars apiece for them. That would give us the money we need to keep Harding quiet."

"Three thousand dollars?"

"Yes, and if we do that we'll still have the rest of the flock left on Wayward Island. If we have a good lambing, we'll soon make up the numbers."

"Whatever you think best, Harry."

"To save time we could take the barge across to the island next weekend and leave it there. Then, when the school holidays start, Meg and Joe could come over with me to lend a hand. They're real sea dogs now, you know. It would only take a day or two."

Joe lay quite still, scarcely breathing. It sounded too good to be true.

"Would you get the money in time to pay Mr. Harding?" Aunt Ellen asked.

"Yes, Herbie says he'll pay cash, so everything will fit in nicely. If we go over to Wayward on the Monday at the start of the school holidays, we'll be back with the sheep by Wednesday, and Harding's deadline is on the Friday."

"But what if you're held up?"

"We'll have time to spare, so don't worry."

Luckily Joe didn't have to nurse his secret for long this time, because Uncle Harry came out into the open with it the following day. Meg whooped with delight. "Mind you," her father said, "we'll have to buckle down because there'll be nobody to help us. Herc's leg is still bad and Boxhead has to help Stewy on *Petrel*. There's nobody else I can hire."

"We can do it," Joe said airily.

His uncle eyed him doubtfully. "It won't be a picnic, Joe. After we've culled out the sheep we want, we'll have to drive them to the landing and load them onto the barge. It'll be hard work."

"We'll take Mophead," Joe said. "He'll be a marvelous help."

Uncle Harry raised one eyebrow. "Help? A hindrance, more likely. He's as silly as a sheep himself."

Joe was hurt. "No, honest. He's really good with sheep. You'll see."

Soon all the arrangements were under way. They towed the barge across to the island on the following Saturday and left it moored safely in Cay Cove. Before returning to Cockle Bay, they counted the sheep, checked the drafting yards, and mended the wooden race, the fenced-in channel that led down to the loading area, so that everything would be ready for them on their next visit.

Back home there were dozens of things to be done. Uncle Harry had a backlog of jobs in the workshop that had to be cleared so that Otto Minz and Aunt Ellen could run the service station again while he was away. Herbie Driver had to be told to be ready with his stock truck as soon as *Seahorse* returned from Wayward Island so that the sheep could be transferred straight from the barge after their sea voyage. Meg and Joe had to help with all the supplies—food for four or five days in case they were held up, tea, coffee, and sugar, spare blankets, kerosene for the lamps, drums of fuel for the engine, rope, twine, tools, warm clothing, and even a few bags of firewood because there was so little natural timber on the island. They would be staying in the old three-room cottage near the landing on the island. There were a few pens and a dilapidated shed nearby.

Uncle Harry was uneasy about making the trip with only Meg and Joe to help him. He would have liked at least one other strong person—a grown-up—but it was impossible to find anyone who had four or five days to spare. And then, on the very last day of the school term, he had a telephone call from Adelaide. It was George Lane on the line saying that he was coming over to Cockle

Bay for ten days to have a final battle with Scarface if a boat could be made available.

When Uncle Harry explained the situation, George Lane said he would make a bargain with him—he would help load the sheep provided he could have five or six days of uninterrupted fishing afterward. Uncle Harry was surprised and delighted. He even agreed that George Lane could troll and prospect for sharks on their way over to Wayward Island on the first morning if he wanted to.

Three big frozen tuna from Mick Mareolas's freezer were therefore hastily added to the cargo, along with all the other paraphernalia that George needed. He arrived in his small private airplane on the Sunday afternoon, landing bumpily in one of the paddocks on Herbie Driver's farm, and saying that he could feel in his bones that this time something exciting and amazing was going to happen.

Joe, helping to lug the big frozen tuna on board *Seahorse* in the gloom before daybreak on Monday morning, paused and wiped his brow. "I reckon this is a messy way of getting lures and bait," he said. "Why don't we just go up to Charlie Chops and buy a dressed sheep or half a bullock?"

George Lane almost had a seizure at the idea. "They're *mammals*," he cried. "We're not allowed to use mammals."

"Why not?"

"It's forbidden. I'd end up in jail if I did."

"Not even old cows or sheep or dead horses?"

"No way. No land mammals, no seals, no porpoises."

"But they're fish."

"Porpoises?" George Lane laughed. "They're mammals, my boy. You'd be in big trouble if you touched one of them."

Joe shook his head in astonishment. "I learn something new every day."

Meg smirked at him. "So you should. It would be a dumb day if you didn't."

Uncle Harry was busy hefting the drums of fuel aboard.

"Are we taking the dinghy, Dad?" Meg asked. It was a small rowboat that they usually towed behind them or even carried perched across the stern.

"No, not when we have to tow the barge on the way back. If we sink, you'll have to use the raft." He was talking about the self-inflating life raft that was kept in a locker near the wheelhouse. He had bought it at a sale of surplus equipment from the Air Force, and luckily he had never had to use it.

Last of all Joe went to get Mophead. He was tied to the handrail at the side of the jetty and was in such a frenzy of excitement that Joe feared he was going to jump off the decking at any minute and strangle himself at the end of his leash.

"Now," said Joe gently as he led him forward, "you be a good boy. Don't get in anyone's way, don't steal meat, and don't fall overboard."

They cast off just before daybreak, waving to Aunt Ellen and Maureen as they slid away from the jetty.

"We'll be back by Thursday at the latest," Uncle Harry shouted. "I'll give Andy Jones a radio call before we leave."

"Good luck," Aunt Ellen called.

8

Instead of steering a straight course for Wayward Island, Uncle Harry swung out in a westerly curve so that *Seahorse* passed near Herringbone Shoals.

"You never know," he said to George Lane. "Scarface could still be hanging about."

George Lane smiled. "I hope so."

As they neared the reef, he hung out the lures and leaned over the transom to set the drip going. Meg and Joe sat in the stern beside him, watching the drips spread miraculously into an oily wake. Mophead was even more interested than they were, and Joe had to keep a firm hold on his leash lest he try to dive overboard.

Uncle Harry now took *Seahorse* on an east-west

traverse for a mile or so and then cut across the oil slick at right angles for several more. Finally he sailed around the whole area in a circle. There was not a shark to be seen.

"I think Scarface has migrated to Western Australia," George Lane said wryly, "and he's taken all his friends with him."

"That's because you gave him a headache last time," Uncle Harry answered. "He's had quite enough of you." He glanced at his watch and stood looking out to sea, squinting at the sharp sheen of the morning sunshine. "The day's still a baby; it's barely eight o'clock. We can scout about for hours yet if you like."

"Yes, but you want to get over to your sheep."

"There's no hurry. It doesn't matter if we don't reach the island until late this afternoon."

George Lane shrugged. "I think you might be burning up a lot of fuel for nothing."

Two or three fishing cutters passed by on their way to the grounds. On the horizon another one was heading back to Cockle Bay with its catch. They all stood well away from *Seahorse* because they knew they wouldn't be very popular if they upset a big-game fisherman at a critical moment.

After a while Uncle Harry swung back on course for Wayward Island. "Let's try farther out," he suggested. "They could be in deeper water."

They sailed on for another hour, and then Uncle Harry started navigating in a weird zigzag pattern, as if *Seahorse* had suddenly become a destroyer trying to avoid a dozen enemy torpedoes. Still they saw nothing. George Lane kept refilling the drip can with oil, and Uncle Harry peered at the fuel gauge and sighed. He had meant to top up the main tank before leaving Cockle Bay, but there had been so many other last-minute jobs to do that he hadn't managed it. He was sure there was enough fuel for a straightforward crossing to Wayward Island, but he hadn't counted on quite so much fruitless shark chasing. Not that it really mattered, because they were carrying plenty of spare gasoline in drums. It was just that refueling at sea was a nuisance, especially in choppy water.

Meg and Joe went down to the galley and came back with hot coffee and crackers for morning tea. They all squeezed into the wheelhouse, where Uncle Harry stood holding the wheel in one hand and his mug of coffee in the other.

"I think you've done your job, Mr. Lane," Joe said. "You've scared them all away—tooth, fin, and tail."

Meg agreed. "I s'pose even sharks get frightened—it's only natural."

George Lane blew on his coffee. "Yes, you may as well head for the island, Harry. We'll try on another day." He was very relaxed. He had put his gear aside and seemed resigned to an uneventful trip to Wayward Island.

Meg's father grunted. "Well, if *you* can't see any,

Meg, nobody can. Your eyes are better than anyone else's."

Another half hour passed. Meg and Joe had nothing to do except do the dishes, amuse Mophead, and wait. And then, as if to prove her father's point, Meg suddenly gave a shout and pointed. "Look. Look there."

"Where?"

"There, there. Out to starboard."

At that moment Joe saw it too—a dark shadow moving very fast under the broken water.

"A big one," Meg called.

"Yes, I see him," her father shouted. "You're right, a really big fellow." He eased *Seahorse* back to an idle, barely enough to hold her bow into the swell.

"Scarface?" Joe asked. Surprisingly, his legs were trembling. "Is it Scarface?"

George Lane was lowering the lures, peering feverishly over the stern. "It's hard to be sure."

"It must be Scarface," Uncle Harry called. "He's being so sly and suspicious."

"In any case he's a monster," George Lane answered. "He's worth a try."

Immediately there was action in every direction. "Meg, come and take the wheel," her father yelled. "And Joe, bring up some chunks of bait. Hurry."

The folding hatch went down, the chair was made secure, the lures were lowered. George Lane hastily buckled on his harness, calling for his rod at the same time. As Uncle Harry came leaping down from the wheelhouse and Joe came rushing up with the bait, they both cannoned into Mophead. "Blast," Uncle Harry yelled. "Take that mutt down below and tie him up. He'll be the death of us."

Reluctantly, Joe did as he was told. "Never mind, Mophead," he said softly, "it's just for an hour or two while we catch this shark."

There was still haste and confusion when he returned to the deck. Nobody had yet been able to catch a glimpse of the shark's face, but George Lane was almost ready and Uncle Harry was frantically baiting the huge hook. *Seahorse* had started to wallow, and he shouted at Meg to push up the engine speed a fraction. There was a sudden surge of power, and he bellowed again: "Not so much, not so much. Cut her back." Everyone was tense.

Suddenly the shark shot in toward them from the rear. It came like lightning, without warning, reared up, and seized the corner of the transom in its jaws. The timber splintered horribly as the shark tore out a jagged piece in one enormous bite. At the same time they all saw its head clearly, and there, as plain as a chalk mark, was the telltale scar on its upper jaw.

Uncle Harry recoiled and George Lane stared incredulously. "Holy Moses," Uncle Harry cried. "Did you see that? He attacked the boat. Scarface actually attacked the boat. Quite deliberately."

"I've heard of sharks doing that," George answered, "but this is the first time I've ever seen it happen."

"You'd swear that he recognized us, that he was trying to take revenge. Like Moby-Dick."

Joe knew the story of Moby-Dick and went white at the thought.

"It's just as well *Seahorse* is as solid as old oak. If we were in a flimsy little boat, I wouldn't feel too comfortable."

"Here he comes again," George Lane called. "Offer him the bait, Harry. Quick."

Uncle Harry swung the big slab of tuna over the side and heaved it toward the dark form as it swept forward. But instead of taking the bait Scarface reared again, seized the beam that held the hanging lures, and wrenched it away like a match.

"Look out," Uncle Harry yelled. "He's got the devil in him. He's fighting mad. He wants to tear us to bits."

"Be ready," George called. "He'll come again in a minute. Let him have the bait early. Throw it out as far as you can." Uncle Harry did as George suggested, just as the shark turned and moved in for the third time. For a breathless second it seemed that Scarface would veer and attack *Seahorse* again elsewhere, but then he speeded up, rolled slightly, and wolfed down the bait.

"Got him!" Uncle Harry's shout was so triumphant that an onlooker would have thought the battle was already over. But it was only just beginning.

The shark ran at once, and the line shrieked off the reel. George Lane was still trying to adjust his position in the chair while hanging on to the rod with both hands. One of the straps of his harness was twisted, and it was pinching his flesh. Everything had been done in such a frenzied rush that they needed a minute or two to settle down.

Uncle Harry was pulling a heavy leather glove onto his right hand. Although the cuts in his palm from his last encounter with Scarface had healed nicely, he was not willing to risk more lacerations today. He eyed George Lane for a minute and then went up to join Meg in the wheelhouse.

"Get ready to back up," he said. "George can't afford to run out much more line."

Meg nodded nervously.

"Keep your eye on George all the time."

"Yes, Dad."

"And watch your engine speed. Ease her in and out of gear, forward or reverse, as you need to. Can you do that?"

"Yes, Dad."

"If you need help, yell right away. I'll be up like a shot."

"Thanks, Dad."

Uncle Harry stood watching for a while, offering advice and even thrusting out his hand to move the controls once or twice until he was certain Meg could cope. Then he went back to George Lane.

The shark began to give ground at last, and George started the long battle to reel it in. Joe felt that he had seen it all before. It was like a slow-motion replay of everything that had happened two or three weeks earlier. There were the same needs and the same requests: a handkerchief to stop the perspiration from running into George's eyes, a damp cloth, a drink of cold water.

George concentrated entirely on the wiles of the shark and the slow grind of the reel—pulling the rod up on a backbreaking haul, letting it dip suddenly, and reeling desperately for a turn or two to take up the slack he had won. Haul—dip—reel, haul—dip—reel, haul—dip—reel.

Uncle Harry kept calling encouragement. "You're gaining on him."

George Lane smiled wryly. "Yes, an inch a minute."

Uncle Harry turned to Joe. "When the time comes, I'll take the trace and I want you to be ready with the gaffs. Hand them to me the moment we get him alongside."

"Yes, Uncle Harry."

"You'd better check them now."

As Joe bent down to pick up the biggest gaff with its wicked hook, he heard George Lane say, "I think I'll put a bit more drag on the reel. Make him work a bit harder." A second later there was an agonized cry followed by a thunderous thump and a splash. There was a moment of stunned silence and then a roaring exclamation from Uncle Harry. "George! George!"

Joe looked up with a jerk. At first he couldn't understand what had happened. The hatch cover was down and Uncle Harry was racing down the deck, stripping off his heavy jacket and yelling at Meg, "Cut the engine, cut the engine." Then he dived headlong into the sea.

Joe was utterly bewildered. He ran up to the wheelhouse, looking about helplessly. "What's up?" he cried. "Whatever's happened?"

Meg was standing horrified, clutching the wheel. "Oh my God" was all she said.

Joe was beside himself. "What's going on?"

"The shark's pulled George overboard. Dad's gone in after him."

Joe couldn't believe his ears. "Pulled him *overboard?*"

Meg pointed at the hatch cover lying in its forward position. "Someone forgot the bolts."

"Holy Moses." In a flash Joe understood everything. In all the haste and turmoil after they had first sighted Scarface, nobody had thought to push in the big barrel bolts that held the hatch cover in position while it was folded back to take the chair. It was free to swing forward like a hinged door, and that was exactly what it had done. As soon as George had increased the drag on the reel, so that the pull of the shark overcame the weight of the hatch, it had swung up and over like an ancient catapult and hurled George straight into the sea. And because he had snapped his reel into its special socket in the harness, he was being towed away to his death.

Joe rushed back to the stern, peering frantically into the shadowy water. "George is still strapped in. He has to break free or he'll drown," he yelled.

"Dad'll unbuckle him."

"If he can find him." Joe gave a sudden gasp and pointed. "Look, look."

Meg's face was ashen. "Oh no."

A swirling red stain was spreading slowly on the surface, ten or twenty yards beyond the boat. "Blood. It's blood, Joe."

Joe's voice shrank to a whisper. "Oh God. Surely the shark hasn't got them, Meg?"

Meanwhile George Lane was fighting for his life. He couldn't remember what had happened, except that his world had disintegrated in an instant. It was as if he had been picked up and hurled over the stern like a cannonball. At the same time he had felt a stunning blow on the side of his head and a vicious cut on his left arm, but he didn't know the cause. It could have been the edge of the platform or a spike of metal, or even the propeller.

Luckily he was still conscious. He knew he was sinking into deeper water and that the reel was still running. When it reached the end of the line, he would simply be towed away by Scarface. He had about thirty seconds to free himself—if he didn't black out in the meantime. He was losing a lot of blood from his nose and the deep cut on his arm, yet he remained calm. "Mustn't panic," he told himself. "Mustn't lose my head." He groped about for the buckles of his harness and managed to snap them open. Then quite deliberately he pushed his rod and reel outward, away from his body. He knew he was throwing away thousands of dollars worth of equipment, but that didn't seem to matter at the moment. As soon as he was free, he started to rise toward the surface as quickly as he could.

Uncle Harry could find nothing at the first try. He came up spluttering, looked about hastily for signs of George, and glanced briefly at Meg and Joe, who were pointing and shouting from the stern of the boat. He couldn't understand what they were saying, and he didn't have time to find out. He took a deep breath and dived again.

"That blood'll bring the sharks around for sure," Joe said in an anguished voice. "They'll go crazy once they get a sniff of it."

"Pray to God there are none about."

"Scarface is."

"I think he'd swim away. He'd be going out to sea."

"Towing George."

They were silent, peering around frantically. "I wish Dad would hurry up," Meg said. "He's only got a minute. God help George if he doesn't find him soon."

As if in answer to Meg's prayer, two heads popped out of the water before them. Uncle Harry was holding George by the shoulders.

"Throw a rope," he yelled. "George has been hurt."

"That's what we tried to tell you," Meg shouted. "There's blood everywhere."

Her father looked about anxiously. "Hurry. We're right in the middle of it."

He seized the rope and looped it under George's armpits. "Quick," he called. "Pull."

It was a clumsy job, but at last, after a lot of grunting and pulling from Meg and Joe, some vigorous shoving from Uncle Harry, and some self-help scrabbling from George, they managed to get their jettisoned fisherman back on board. He winced at the pressure on his lacerated arm, and he put his right hand over the wound to try to stanch the blood. Shortly afterward Uncle Harry heaved himself up over the transom like a porpoise and lay in the stern, with water streaming from him.

George gave a weak smile. "Thanks," he said. "That's the first time I've ever made shark bait of myself."

"Not a nice feeling," answered Uncle Harry, getting slowly to his feet.

"You had ten seconds to spare," Joe called. "Look." He pointed over the port side to where two big sharks were circling at high speed. Their snouts seemed to be thrust forward, for all the world like bloodhounds sniffing out a scent. "They've found the blood."

"I'm glad we missed their luncheon appointment," George Lane answered.

Meg gazed at the sharks and shuddered. "Imagine being mauled by one of them."

Uncle Harry turned to George Lane, who was sitting limply on the deck. "Now, some bandages for those gashes and then a quick trip back to the Bay. You're going to need stitches."

"There isn't time for you to do that," George answered. "You should be on your way to the island."

"Rubbish," Uncle Harry replied. He turned to Meg and Joe. "Get the first-aid kit. And you, Meg, tear one of the pillowcases into strips. We have to stop this bleeding." As he hurried below with Meg, Joe heard the engine start and felt the bow lift as *Seahorse* went onto full power.

Fortunately they didn't have to go far after all. As they neared Herringbone Shoal, Mick Mareolas came sailing across their bows in his new boat, *Athena*, heading for home. "I can go with him," George said. "It'll save you making an unnecessary trip."

Uncle Harry was doubtful. "Are you sure?"

"Sure I'm sure."

They hailed Mick on the radio and told him the details of the accident. He brought *Athena* alongside, and there were a few tricky moments while George was transferred from one vessel to the other—the two boats wallowing side by side and everyone yelling instructions. They managed it at last, and Uncle Harry shouted above the slopping of the sea against the hulls. "Ellen will run you up to Ceduna to have that arm stitched."

George Lane waved weakly. "Thanks, Harry."

"Don't thank me. I'm the idiot who should have checked the barrel bolts."

"We'll remember next time."

"When will that be?"

George shrugged. "I won't be able to use this arm for a while, so I'll fly back to Adelaide in a day or two."

"Okay, we'll be in touch."

"Sorry I can't help you with the sheep."

"Don't worry, we'll manage."

"See you then."

Athena headed away at full speed toward the north, and *Seahorse* turned south and made for Wayward Island. Uncle Harry looked at his watch. "We won't bother about lunch until we reach the cove," he said. "We should be there by one o'clock." He glanced at the fuel gauge and wrinkled his nose. "That is, if we don't run dry beforehand. All this hide-and-seek with Scarface has almost drained the fuel tank."

Joe looked at the needle. It was hovering on zero. "But you can refuel at sea, can't you?"

"Oh yes, but I like to avoid it if I can."

"And what about Scarface now?" Joe asked.

Uncle Harry smiled. "The gods must be on his side. I think he's fated to be free."

Joe looked out toward Wayward Island. Its higher bluffs were just visible on the horizon. At the sight of it he tingled with pleasure and excitement—as he always did. "What are we going to do this afternoon?" he asked.

"Get things ready. We'll load the sheep tomorrow or Wednesday, depending on the weather."

Uncle Harry called Meg to take over the wheel again while he went below to change. Joe set Mophead free and watched Meg enviously out of the corner of his eye. He would have given an eyetooth for a turn in the wheelhouse, but he realized that Meg had a much stronger claim than he did. After all, she was Uncle Harry's daughter and she had spent years sailing about in boats while he was still riding trains and trolleys in Melbourne. But someday he would get his chance. He hoped it would be soon.

They heard Uncle Harry on the radio, first calling VH6BA repeatedly and then giving Andy Jones the news about the accident.

"Ask Ellen to stand by to run George Lane up to the doctor. He'll need a few stitches."

"Roger, Harry. How is he?"

"He'll be okay. Just a bit groggy. Lost a lot of blood."

"Right, I'll have someone waiting."

"Thanks Andy. And tell Ellen everything else is okay with us. Meg and Joe are as fit as fiddles. We're off to the island now. We should be back by Wednesday night or Thursday morning at the latest. I'll give you a call when we're ready to sail, together with an E.T.A. Okay?"

"Roger, Harry. Have a good time."

They heard the click of the switches as Uncle Harry finished the call. "Well, that's that," he said. "Now we can get on with the job we set out to do."

9

Uncle Harry had a theory that accidents always came in pairs. "Every disaster travels with a mate," he said. "If you ever have an accident, watch out for another one coming in the opposite direction."

Meg had a twinkle in her eyes as she pulled on her cap. "Some people say that all accidents are caused by people—like the way someone forgot the barrel bolts on the hatch cover this morning."

Her father snorted. "The less said about that, the better. George Lane and I will never live it down."

To Joe, sitting in the stern with his hand on Mophead's collar, nothing seemed more remote than accidents. He felt contented and relaxed. The island was there again right before his eyes, growing clearer all the time. It reminded him of a whale—the granite head of Black Bluff in the west, the fluked tail in the east, the undulating backbone, the water catchment, the salty samphire inlets, the bony reefs, Cay Cove and the hill beyond it, the hollow where the cottage crouched, sheltered from the wind. He had been there only twice before, but it had been love at first sight.

"It's a beautiful place," he said softly. "It really is."

Meg peered at him closely and grinned. "Don't tell me you're going all droopy and dreamy about it again."

"I can't help it. It gets to me."

She smiled warmly. "I know. And loading a hundred sheep will get to you too, especially to your back."

They were only about a mile offshore now. *Seahorse* was surging forward lustily, rising and falling smoothly with the swell. Everything seemed right with the world. And then, without warning, the engine stopped.

"Blast it." Uncle Harry looked as if he wanted to take off his cap and jump on it. "We're out of gas—and within a kick of the cove." But he controlled his temper and became very businesslike. He glanced at the shore, looked quickly over the side, and started giving orders.

"Joe, let the anchor go. Make it quick. You help him, Meg." He watched them as they ran to the bow. "It should bite, all right; there's only forty or fifty feet of water here."

As the anchor chain rattled out, he was already unscrewing the cap from the fuel tank.

"Is the anchor holding?" he called a minute later.

Joe peered hard. "I think it is—the chain's taut."

"Keep an eye on it. The tide's running in. We don't want to finish up on the rocks."

He took the hand pump and fitted it to the first of the spare drums. "Look out, muttonhead," he growled as Mophead accidentally got in his way. There was a moment's delay before the pump was primed, and then they heard the gurgle of gas tumbling into the tank and smelled the richly sweet tang of the fumes.

"Better stay there, Joe," he shouted without looking up, "just in case you have to let out a bit more chain. And Meg, pop into the wheelhouse and give a yell the moment you think she's drifting. You can see better from up there."

Joe never forgot what happened next. It would become burned into his memory for the rest of his life. He was bending over the chain at the bow, looking back to acknowledge what Uncle Harry had just said. Meg was walking along the deck with one finger on the handrail, making for the wheelhouse. And Mophead was near the stern wagging his tail and watching Uncle Harry intently as he worked. And in that second the whole world seemed to blow up.

There was an enormous explosion and a terrifying sheet of flame. It was a thunderous sound, like a bomb half buried in the ground, and the flame was an inferno—a fiery upheaval shot through with surges of red and orange, rushing upward and outward with the fury of an atomic blast. Joe, crouching at the very tip of the bow had a momentary glimpse of Uncle Harry hurled backward with his cap blown from his head and his hands jerking upward like the limbs of a rag doll.

At the same time, Meg lifted her hand to her head, as if someone had just struck her a savage blow across the face. Then she reeled back and, partly falling and partly flung, disappeared over the side. A second later the whole of the rear half of the boat was a holocaust.

Joe's brain seemed slow to react, but in reality a dozen horrors raced through his mind in the blink of an eye. The gasoline had exploded. Something had ignited it—the hot engine, an incandescent fragment, static electricity, an accidental spark from two pieces of metal striking together . . . There was no time to think about it—no time and no point. Uncle Harry was in the sea somewhere, probably badly hurt; Meg had gone overboard too and there was no sign of her. The boat was a raging furnace and there were likely to be more explosions at any minute.

His first impulse was to leap, to escape the flames. But then the three of them would be in the water without support, a mile from shore, with Uncle Harry and Meg injured and he, Joe, the weakest swimmer of them all. He doubted whether he could reach the island by himself, let alone if he had to support someone else. And there were sharks.

Although an outsider might have thought he was making conscious decisions, he really acted by instinct. With a gasp he sprang forward toward the locker of the life raft they had joked about that very morning. The wheelhouse shielded him from the worst of the heat, although the glass panes were beginning to shatter above his head.

The locker had a hinged door that opened outward and was kept in place by a brass hasp and staple. He lunged at the bolt, wrenching it out and hurling it away in one movement. But the hasp itself, stiff with paint and age, refused to budge. He jammed his fingers behind it and heaved with both hands, tearing one of his fingernails to the quick as his grip slipped. Blood oozed from the wound but he didn't even notice it. He seized his pocketknife from his jacket and, cupping it in the palm of his hand, smashed it down desperately on the hasp. It moved. He struck again and yet again, shattering the handle of his knife but edging the hasp forward bit by bit. Thumping and clawing, he forced it away at last and the door fell open. The life raft lay inside. As he seized it and leaped back, he was vaguely aware of a block of print in bold red lettering:

TO INFLATE PULL TOGGLE
WARNING:
DO NOT INFLATE IN CONFINED SPACE.

If he had been able to absorb the message properly, he would have laughed at the ridiculousness of it. There was nothing very confined about the Antarctic Ocean between Wayward Island and the mainland. He pulled the small red handle, simultaneously flinging the whole thing away from him into the sea. Then he followed it overboard in a clumsy dive. As he hit the water, he was aware of another tremendous explosion behind him, and a rush of heat about his body. When he surfaced a couple of seconds later, *Seahorse* looked like a funeral pyre. Huge columns of flame and smoke were belching into the sky. Part of the wheelhouse had been blown away, and the whole of the stern was lying in a lake of burning gasoline.

Joe took in everything at a glance. The raft had inflated miraculously and was bobbing jauntily a few yards beyond the bow. Meg had somehow appeared off the starboard side. She was supporting her father, swimming hard to tow him farther away from the burning boat. He seemed to be conscious, because he was trying to help himself, moving one arm weakly in a paddling motion.

For a moment Joe's terrors receded a little. At least they were alive. He hailed Meg. "Hey, are you all right?"

She paused, treading water and wiping her eyes

quickly with one hand. "Dad's hurt but I'm okay."

"Are you sure?"

"Yes. Something clobbered me on the side of the face. I think I've got a black eye."

He was concerned and started splashing toward her. "No, no." She waved him away. "Go after the raft. Grab it while you can. If there's a gust of wind, you'll never catch up with it."

He felt like a jerk for not having realized that before. "Sorry," he said apologetically. He turned and swam toward the raft as hard as he could.

"Hurry," she called after him. "I don't think I can hold Dad much longer."

The raft was as skittish as a colt. It bobbed and veered and spun infuriatingly to the motion of the waves. Trying to get a grip on it was like trying to pick up a wet melon seed. Joe pushed and nudged and butted it, hoping to maneuver it toward Meg and her father. It was hopeless. He was getting tired, and he knew he would not be able to keep up his frenzied shepherding much longer. When he glimpsed a pair of short paddles strapped inside the raft, he decided that he would have to try to board it.

In a desperate move he heaved himself upward and forward, flinging his arms over the curved sides of the raft, clutching for a handhold. He was lucky. Grips had been molded into the rubber-and-plastic lining, and he was able to hold on. Scrabbling and straining, he slowly wriggled his body forward until his right knee cleared the side. Then, with a strong thrust, he toppled forward and lay prostrate in the bottom of the raft.

"Made it," he gasped.

He wrenched one of the paddles free, knelt near the side of the raft, and paddled urgently. Even now the task was anything but easy. The raft still refused to behave itself, and he could see that Meg was almost exhausted. Fortunately her father was conscious and had a little of his strength. "This way," she called. "Quick, Joe."

As he neared her, he was about to jump overboard to help but she stopped him. "No, no, stay where you are. Kneel down again and see if you can grab Dad by the arms."

He managed it at last, although it was incredibly difficult because of the bucking motion of the sea. "Hang on," Meg gasped. "Don't let him go, whatever you do."

"I've got him," Joe said firmly. He tried to sound much braver than he really felt.

"Now," Meg called. "Can you pull him forward?"

Joe hauled with all his strength, but as soon as his uncle's body rose clear of the buoyant water, it felt like a ton of lead.

"You pull and I'll push," Meg shouted.

"Okay."

"Ready?"

They struggled furiously, but it was hopeless.

"Leave my hands free, Joe." The voice was little more than a croak, and for a second Joe scarcely realized that it was his uncle who was speaking. Joe hastily adjusted his grip, clutching Uncle Harry under the armpits.

"Try again."

"Ready?"

"Now."

It was not Joe or Meg but Uncle Harry himself who achieved the miracle. By some superhuman effort of his will he managed to get his arms over the side and haul himself forward until Joe, straining with gritted teeth, finally toppled him into the raft beside him. Then Joe turned quickly, took Meg firmly by the hands, and helped her scramble aboard as well.

"We've done it," she said, panting and spluttering. "We've done it."

Joe was now able to see Uncle Harry clearly for the first time. His face, arms, and hands were burned. His eyebrows and eyelashes were gone, and most of the hair had been scorched from his head. His trousers and jacket were the color of old charcoal, charred and burned into ashy strips. Even his shoes were gone. Looking at him lying there, Joe trembled to think what he might be suffering—whether the blazing clothes had burned through to the flesh, whether the blast had caused other injuries, whether he had breathed in gasoline fumes and drawn the fire into his nose, throat, and lungs.

Meg was bending over him. "Dad. Dad, are you all right?"

He took a little while to answer. "Burns," he said simply. "Gas burns. Knocked me about a bit." He almost managed a cracked sort of smile.

It encouraged her. "We'll get you ashore," she said softly.

He eyed Joe with a strange lidless stare. "Had to use the old raft after all," he croaked.

"Joe managed to get it," she said. "Just in time."

"Good work, Joe."

She propped him up as best she could with his head resting on the side of the raft. Joe took off his waterlogged jacket, hastily squeezed it, and rolled it into a makeshift pillow. He sat watching while Meg adjusted it to cushion her father against the jolting action of the waves. She was drawing in her breath with a hissing sound while she worked, and he suddenly realized that she was not doing it from exertion or fear but from pain. The left side of her face from chin to forehead was one enormous bruise, and her eye was partly closed by the swelling. Her woollen cap was missing, and her soft hair was singed, blackened, and shriveled at the ends. It stank of burning.

"Meg, are you sure you're okay?" he asked again anxiously.

She brushed his question aside. "Yeah, yeah. I've got a throb like an engine in my head, that's all. It must have been a bit of wood or something, blown out by the blast."

"Lucky you weren't any closer."

She picked up the second paddle. "Come on, let's try to get ashore."

It was hard work. The raft behaved like a bumper car, turning and dipping every which way until they learned to paddle more rhythmically, like a couple of Indians in a canoe. Luckily the breeze and the tide were both running in their favor, and so they made good progress, even though their navigation was as crooked as an arthritic finger.

They stood well away from the burning boat now. Uncle Harry could do nothing but stare at it with his seared eyes and croak, "Oh God, oh God," over and over again. For *Seahorse* was nothing but a foundering wreck, burned to the waterline, belching smoke rather than fire and settling slowly at her mooring. The second explosion from the spare fuel drums had clearly blown out some of her timbers, and she was sinking by the stern. The column of smoke rose up and slanted away on the breeze. They rested on their paddles for a moment, watching sadly. "It looks like the smoke from the town dump," Meg said bitterly. "No better than a floating bonfire."

Whether it was the mention of the dump that

stung Joe's memory he was never able to say, but he suddenly swung around in horror. "Mophead," he cried. "Where's Mophead?"

Meg was just as shocked as he was. "He . . . he wasn't still tied up, was he?"

"No, no. He was free."

"Are you sure?"

"I untied him myself. Don't you remember right at the end? He kept getting in your dad's way."

She remembered. "Poor Mophead."

Joe was distraught. "We have to go back; he could still be alive."

"Not on the boat, he couldn't."

"In the water then."

"We would have seen him."

"We have to look for him all the same."

She lifted her bruised head and faced him squarely. "We'd never row this thing against the wind and tide, Joe. And we've got Dad to think of."

He opened his mouth to shout at her, but then he saw her father gazing at him in a dazed way and changed his mind. "Oh Mophead," he said softly.

"He's gone, Joe."

Joe looked away quickly. His face and his hair were still dripping with water, so it was hard to know whether his eyes were wet from seawater or tears.

"Row, Joe. We have to get Dad ashore."

They were cold and starting to shiver. Joe's hands trembled. The wind froze his flesh through his wet clothes, just as the thought of Mophead lying dead in the sea somewhere froze his heart.

There were a few feverish moments as they neared the channel through the reef. Twice the raft was almost swept up on the rocks by a surging wave, but each time Meg and Joe were able to prevent disaster by a combination of rowing and desperate fending with their paddles. And so at last they brought their unpredictable craft past the two little flat-topped islands that guarded the safe water of Cay Cove. There they ignored the wooden landing, because it stood too high out of the water for the raft, and paddled on until they grounded gently on the beach beyond.

Uncle Harry, who had been lolling back stupefied, opened his eyes when he felt the sand grating underneath. "Well done," he croaked weakly. He made a movement as if to try to stand up, but groped about dizzily and flopped back on his haunches.

"Don't, Dad," Meg cried. "Leave it to us. We'll get you out." She jumped ashore and turned to Joe. "Come on. Let's pull the raft as far up the beach as we can."

They both heaved and tugged but didn't get far. Joe looked about despairingly. It was clear that they would never be able to carry a solid man like Meg's father all the way up to the cottage unless they had something like a sled or a platform on wheels. Uncle Harry saw him and guessed what he was thinking.

"The wool cart," he gasped. "Up in the shed."

"I'll get it," Joe called to Meg. "You stay here with your dad." He tore off up the slope past the cottage to the sheep pens and the old shearing shed. He saw the cart as soon as he burst through the door—a low metal platform with a steel handle and four broad-rimmed iron wheels that was used to move the bales of wool down to the landing. It was primitive but effective. He seized the handle and lumbered off with it back to the beach.

Ten minutes later he and Meg finally dragged their patient through the cottage door and eased him onto a bunk in the bedroom. Joe was uncertain about what to do next, but Meg worked like a practiced nurse. In the corner was a big old-fashioned wardrobe, with a tight-fitting door and a key like a jailer's, where her father kept emergency supplies of old bedding in case they were ever marooned on the island by bad weather. Meg seized some clean blankets and sheets and went over to the bunk.

"Dad," she said gently, "we've got to get you into clean clothes. We have to see whether you're burned under your coat and pants."

He nodded. Joe was terribly afraid of what they might find. Already Uncle Harry's face was a dreadful sight—the skin inflamed and the lips swollen. If the flames had gone all the way through the cloth, he would have similar burns, or even worse, on his shoulders and legs and body. He was also starting to suffer from shock, his limbs trembling and his teeth chattering.

To their great relief the burns under the clothing were not bad—a few small patches on the chest and two nasty ones on the legs between the ankle and the knee, where gas must have spewed upward. That was bad enough, of course, but it could have been so much worse. The violent way in which Uncle Harry had been catapulted backward into the sea seemed to have saved him from much more hideous burns, because the water had doused the flames before they could reach his flesh.

When he was safely bedded down between clean sheets, Meg adjusted the blankets to keep him warm. She bent over him. "How are you now, Dad?"

He took a deep breath. "Thanks dear. I'll cope."

She was not convinced. "It's bad, isn't it?"

"The pain's bad. It's really starting to bite."

She was out in the kitchen in an instant, rummaging about in an old cupboard. "I'm sure we had some painkillers in here once," she said to Joe. "Some aspirin or something."

"Bottle or packet?"

"Packet—with each pill wrapped in silver foil."

"I know the sort."

Meg found them, at last, under a half-empty carton of matchboxes. She hurried in to her father with two pills and a glass of water. "Here, take these."

He grinned wearily as he slowly raised his head. "Thanks, Nurse Blake."

She straightened the covers again and tiptoed out of the room like a mother who has tucked in her child. "Try to get some sleep."

Joe was waiting in the kitchen. "Shouldn't we put something on those burns—some ointment or butter or something?"

She was horrified. "Not on burns. Nothing fatty or greasy, even if we had it."

"Why not?"

"That's the worst thing you can do."

"I thought it would help."

"No way. Not fatty things."

Joe was willing to leave it to Meg. "You know more than I do," he said simply.

She picked up the painkillers and broke out a tablet from the foil. "I think I'll take one of these things myself. My head feels as if it's full of rocks."

He watched her, suddenly feeling very helpless. "Shouldn't you be going to bed too?" he asked. "You're not well either." The whole world seemed to have collapsed about his ears. While they had been fighting for their lives, and battling to bring Uncle Harry ashore, there hadn't been time to think. But now he was at a standstill. He looked at his watch. At least it was still working, so the notice on the back cover—"stainless steel, waterproof"—must be true.

"It's two o'clock," he said. "We're late for lunch."

She laughed cynically. "We'll be late for tea and breakfast too, many times over."

He looked at her, slowly realizing what she was saying. "There's nothing to eat, is there? It was all on the boat."

"Everything."

"And there's no way we can get help. No radio or anything."

She shook her head. "No way."

"All we can do is wait."

She sat down, touching the bruise on her face gingerly with her left hand. "Yes, wait. And nobody's going to bother about us for at least three days. There's no reason anyone should think we might be in any trouble at all."

10

It took some time for Joe to comprehend their awful predicament. Everything they depended on had been destroyed with *Seahorse*—food, clothing, tools, kerosene for the lamps, even firewood. Above all, they had lost their only means of contact with the mainland—the radio—and they had heard Uncle Harry himself telling Andy Jones that he wouldn't bother to get in touch with him again until they were loaded and ready to leave on Wednesday night or Thursday morning. And today was only Monday.

It was not just a question of starving for three or four days. Uncle Harry needed a doctor urgently. For the moment he seemed to have survived the disaster, but what if he grew worse during the night, or in the morning, or the day after that? What if an infection set in? What if his lungs had been seared by the blast and he started coughing up blood? Even Meg needed a doctor. Her cheek looked like a huge overripe plum and her left eye was almost completely closed. She was suffering mildly from shock too, but she refused to lie down. Instead she humored him, saying there were a dozen things to do.

"What things?" he asked hopelessly.

"In three or four hours it'll be dark."

"So?"

"So we have to be ready. We have to see whether there's anything in the cupboards, how much kerosene is left in the lamps, how much firewood there is. We have to get rescue signals ready. We have to watch Dad and keep him warm. But first we have to dry our clothes, or we'll both get pneumonia and that'll be the end of everything."

"But we haven't got anything else to wear."

She was impatient. "Then we'll have to improvise, won't we?"

"Oh, sure," he answered peevishly. Sometimes she irritated him so much that he could happily have kicked her in the shins.

"Can you light a fire?" she asked.

"Don't ask stupid questions. Of course I can."

She ignored his rudeness. "Then light one in here."

"In the fireplace?"

"No, on the kitchen table."

"Oh, don't be ridiculous."

Almost at once he regretted what he'd said. She was hurt and in a lot of pain, and he was asking silly questions.

She relented too. "I'm sorry," she exclaimed at exactly the same moment as he said the same thing. They laughed. "So we're both sorry," she said.

"I'd better look for some wood." He made for the door.

"There's a bit left over from last time, around the side of the house. You can use that for starters."

"Okay. What are you going to do?"

"Change."

He brought in the wood and started the fire. There was hardly any paper, so he had to whittle off a few shavings with his broken knife and coax the first little flames very carefully. Fortunately there were plenty of matches. He heard Meg moving about in the third room of the cottage, which was usually used by workmen like Herc when they came over to help with the shearing or fencing. Shortly afterward she emerged dressed in a towel and a large pair of trousers so stiff with age and cobwebs that they almost stood up on their own. The crotch was down between her knees, and the cuffs had been turned up so far that the legs were almost inside out. She had cut a hole in the middle of the towel and put her head through it, draping the ends down her chest and back and tucking it into the top of the trousers. An old piece of rope was tied tightly around her waist to keep the trousers up. With no eyebrows, singed hair, and an enormous bruise on her face, she looked like a clown at a Halloween party.

"Holy Moses," Joe blurted. "Where did you find those?"

"The pants?"

"Yes."

"Hanging on the back of the door. They've been there for twenty years."

Joe's eyes twinkled. "They're probably full of spiders."

"No, I've killed them all."

She was carrying her wet clothing in a sodden bundle. "We'll rinse our clothes in fresh water to get rid of the salt and hang them outside for a while. Later on we'll bring them all in and finish drying them by the fire."

Joe hesitated. She stood by the door and waved him away. "Go on, go on. Your turn."

"But I haven't got anything else to put on."

"There's an old pair of overalls in there, about the same size as these pants. Wear them." She fixed him with a glare from her uninjured eye and went outside.

The overalls were rather like a small tent, but by rolling up the legs and tying off the shoulder straps at half their length, he was able to make do. He followed Meg's example by using a towel to keep his torso warm. Then he hastily rinsed his sea-sodden clothes in a bucket of fresh water from the tank, wrung them as dry as he could, and hung them on the drooping clothesline near the kitchen.

When he went back inside, Meg was busy emptying every box and cupboard in the place. "Matches," she said triumphantly, holding up the carton.

"I know. I've used them already."

"And there are knives, forks, cups, saucers, plates, pots, and plenty of spoons."

"That's good. I like spoons for breakfast," Joe replied. "But I prefer forks for lunch and knives for tea."

She ignored his sarcasm and went straight on. "Breadboard but no bread, butter dish but no butter, sugar bowl but no sugar."

"Just what I like best—nice clean empty dishes."

"And last of all," she said proudly, hiding something behind her back, "three beautiful surprises."

"What?"

"Da-da, da-da." She gave a little fanfare and held up her treasures. "One box of tea, one can of condensed milk, and one candle."

"Great."

"Better than nothing."

Lastly she gathered the three kerosene lamps from the various rooms and measured the amount of fuel in each of them. "Not much kerosene," she said gloomily. "About half a tank all together."

"We'll just have to manage without the lamps."

"We'll put it all together in one lamp and use it in Dad's room. That and the candle. In here we'll have to use the light from the fire."

"If we've got enough wood."

"That's the next thing. Take the axe and scrounge as much as you can."

"Where from?"

"Anywhere. Chop up some of the posts from the sheep pens if you have to—from the middle, where it doesn't matter."

Joe was appalled. "But . . ."

"Go on, for heaven's sake. We can always bring over new posts from the mainland."

He was abashed and set off hastily.

"I'll come and help you as soon as I've finished putting out an S.O.S. message."

He paused and looked back in surprise. "An S.O.S.?"

"Yes."

"Where?"

"Here, in front of the house. A big one on this flat patch of grass."

"What with?"

"Anything. Old sheets, towels, bits of board, iron, broken glass. As long as someone can see it from the air. I'll scratch another one in the sand down by the landing."

"But there aren't any spotter planes. The tuna season's over."

"It's worth a try. There might be a helicopter from

the oil rig. George Lane might even come out for a last look if he's flying back to Adelaide tomorrow."

Joe nodded. Meg, he admitted, was far ahead of him in her thinking. By the time the sun was about to set, they had finished most of their jobs. There was a heap of firewood near the door—most of it from old posts and rails—and an S.O.S. sign in letters ten feet wide on the grass nearby. A distress flag was fluttering from a pole on the chimney. They had brought in the clothes from the line and were drying them out finally in front of the fire.

Meg had dragged a bunk into the kitchen, saying that she would sleep there all night so that she could be near her father. Joe could use the spare room. Then they boiled water in the kettle and made some tea, ladling out a precious dash of condensed milk into each mug. Normally Joe hated tea, but when there was nothing else to eat or drink, it had a wonderful mental effect. It somehow persuaded his stomach that it was having its hot evening meal. So he cupped his hands around the mug to share its warmth, blew on it briskly and unnecessarily, and sipped slowly to prolong the drink as long as he could.

Meg took the third mug and walked quietly into the next room with it. "A cup of tea, Dad?" She asked softly.

Her father looked up. "That you, my girl?" he croaked.

"I've brought you some tea."

He frowned and tried to focus his gaze on her. "Your face," he said. "What on earth have you done to your face?"

"The explosion, Dad, remember?"

He seemed to be disoriented, his mind out of kilter. She wondered if he was really only half conscious.

"Would you like a cup of tea?"

She sat on the bedside and tried to hold the cup to his swollen lips. He sipped and coughed and sipped again. Before long he pushed it aside. "Hurts my mouth," he said. She brought in two more pain-killing tablets from the kitchen and watched while he swallowed them slowly with a bit more tea.

"It hurts, doesn't it?" she asked. "Bad?"

"Burns are bad."

"Maybe the painkillers will help."

"Maybe."

"Try to rest."

She got up and tiptoed out of the room again. Joe watched her as she sat down beside the fire. She was crying so softly that for a minute he wasn't even aware of it until he saw her shoulders shake and heard a sob. "Meg," he said, "why don't you lie down for a while?"

She looked up, her back hunched in misery. "We've got to get help, Joe," she said. "Dad's really bad, and he's going to get worse. We've just got to get help."

Joe had never felt so helpless. "What can we do? Nothing. Nothing except wait until your mom or Andy Jones gets worried and sends someone over. And that won't be until Thursday or Friday."

"That'll be too late."

They stared at one another despairingly. "If only we had a radio," Joe said. "Or even a signal of some sort—a rocket."

Meg sat forward suddenly. "A signal. Joe, you're a genius."

Although he felt pleased at her praise, he was still nonplussed. "But we haven't got a signal."

"We'll make one."

"How?"

"With the lamp and a box."

Joe couldn't picture what she was talking about.

"And a shutter," she said.

"A what?"

"A shutter of some kind. We'll make an Aldis lamp."

At last he began to understand. He knew what an Aldis lamp was and he had read stories about their use on warships.

"Moses," he said. "D'you think it would work?"

"We'll make it work."

She stood up and started rummaging around, peering into every corner with her one eye like a shortsighted terrier. There were no suitable boxes or cans, but in the end she found a strong carton with the top cut on three sides so that it swung like a hinged lid. "This'll do," she said. "The lid'll be the shutter."

"You're ahead of me," he said. "How the heck is that going to work?"

She was impatient. "Like this." She seized the carton and let it lie on its side. "You stand the lamp in it when it's lying in this position. Then you just lift up the lid to let the light shine out and swing it down to cut it off again."

"I'm starting to see the light."

She jerked her head in disgust at his pun. "Lord save us."

"A blinking light will be better than a steady one."

"Of course. It'll blink out S.O.S."

He looked at her in astonishment. "S.O.S.?"

"Yes, you jerk. In Morse."

"Morse?"

"Sure. Morse code."

"How do you do that?"

"With three dots, three dashes, and three dots. Like this." She tapped on the table with the handle of a knife, calling the code as she did so. "Dot-dot-dot, dash-dash-dash, dot-dot-dot."

He was impressed. "I didn't know that."

"Well, you do now."

"And it's the same with a light—short flashes and long flashes?"

"Sure." She turned the carton toward him and

swung the lid up and down three times as quickly as she could. "'Dot-dot-dot. Just like that. Then three slower swings so that the light shines out a bit longer each time for the dashes, and last of all three more short flashes for the final dots."

"How did you learn all that?"

"All what?"

"This stuff about Aldis lamps and Morse code?"

She shrugged. "Everybody here knows that. All the skippers have to—in case their radios fail. You don't think Dad would have taken me out on his boat if I couldn't even send an S.O.S.? You can do it with a flashlight."

He eyed the box approvingly. "I reckon it would work—as long as there was someone out there to see it."

She agreed. "That's the catch. This lamp won't shine very far."

"We could turn it up really high—the wick, I mean."

She shook her head. "No, it'll smoke like mad and use up too much kerosene. You'll blacken the glass and then it won't shine at all."

Joe sighed. "Then we need a reflector—a mirror or something."

She glanced at him admiringly. "Sometimes you're brilliant, Joe. That's a marvelous idea."

She went over and took down the old mirror that was hanging from a hook near the kitchen door. It was the only one in the place except for a tarnished piece fixed onto the door of the bedroom wardrobe.

"That's too big," Joe said. "It'll never fit into the box."

They measured it roughly. It was just the right width but twice as long as it should have been.

"We'll have to break it in half," Meg said.

Joe scoffed. "If you hit it with a hammer or something, you'll smash it into a million bits."

She grinned. "Don't try to teach your cousin to suck eggs." She took a piece of string, dipped it in the fuel tank of the lamp, and tied it neatly around the middle of the mirror. Then she struck a match and lit the kerosene-soaked string. It flared up all around in a smoky flame for a minute or two and finally fell away in strands of ash. As the last bit of flame petered out, Meg lifted the mirror and plunged it into the tub of cold rinsing water that stood by the door. The glass broke neatly in halves.

Joe was astonished. "Gosh, Meg, how did you get to know a thing like that?"

She grunted as she polished one of the pieces with a rag and fitted it into the box. "That's an old country trick. We use it to take the tops off bottles so that we can use them for pickles and homemade jam."

Next she polished the lamp glass until it gleamed in the firelight, and then cut a small hole in the carton above the spot where the lamp was going to stand, so that the smoke and fumes could escape. Last of all she lit the wick and pushed the lamp into position.

"There," she said, swinging the lid up and down. "That's the Special Patent Blake Signaling Lamp."

"It works," he said enthusiastically. "It looks exactly as if the light is blinking on and off. The mirror really makes it flash."

"Good. It ought to be visible for a few miles, don't you think?" She pulled the lamp forward and blew out the flame.

"Farther than that."

"It would be better still if the land here weren't so low. Even the knoll behind the house is nothing but a pimple."

"Yes, it needs higher ground."

"A lot higher. Like a beacon."

He turned toward her suddenly. "What about the headland—Black Bluff? They could almost see it from the mainland then, I reckon."

"That would be perfect—like a little lighthouse. But who's going to go up there in the middle of the night?"

"I will."

As soon as he had said it, he regretted opening his mouth. What on earth was he saying? Who in his right mind would want to go up to the edge of those fearful cliffs in the cold and dark, trying to flash a pitiful little signal into the night? Yet once he had committed himself, he couldn't renege. He very much wanted Meg to think well of him, but if he went back on his word, she would think he was a coward and a fool.

She turned toward him in amazement. "Will you? Really?"

He gulped. "Sure."

She sensed his dread. "It'll be cold and lonely up there, Joe—and dangerous. We can take turns if you like."

"No," he said, desperately defending his pride, "you have to stay here. You have to be with your father."

She glanced quickly at the door of the bedroom. "Yes, I'd better. He should really be having plenty of fluid, and I think he should be exercising his arms and legs every so often."

"How do you know that?"

"I read it somewhere. He should be in the hospital having drips and injections and things."

"For the burns?"

"Yes." She hesitated and then asked a curious question. "Joe, how much of Dad's skin do you think has been burned?"

"What do you mean?"

"What percentage of it?"

"Not much." He thought for a minute. "His face, neck, hands, some on his legs, and a bit on his chest and shoulders. His pants and heavy jacket shielded the rest."

"How much?"

"Ten or fifteen percent."

She seemed relieved. "Are you sure?"

"It wouldn't be any more than that. Probably less. Why?"

"Because if it were thirty or forty percent he would probably die."

Joe looked away. "It's not as much as that, nothing like it." He thought for a moment and added a new thought. "I reckon the burns are not very deep either—just on the surface. He was pitched into the water so fast that he didn't have time to be badly burned."

She put some more wood on the fire to give more light. "I hope you're right, Joe."

He went over to the box with the lamp in it. "You stay with him. I'll go up to the headland."

He practiced flipping the lid up and down. "Dot-dot-dot, dash-dash-dash, dot-dot-dot. Is that about right?"

She smiled. "That'll do. It doesn't matter if it's a bit ragged. If you keep repeating it often enough, any ship that sees it is sure to get the message."

"What'll they do then? Radio?"

"If it's a local boat, they'll let Cockle Bay know, and if it's a big cargo ship they'll radio Adelaide or Melbourne and let them know there's a distress signal on Wayward Island. They'll relay it on."

She picked up his dry clothes from the bunk by the fire. "Here, put these on. You'd better take my coat too, as well as your own, and I'll get you the old blanket from the spare bed. It'll be as cold as an iceberg up there on the bluff."

He went to blunder off into the other room but suddenly realized that it was darker than pitch and there were no lights. She lit the candle from a burning sliver in the fireplace and went to get the blanket. When she returned, she filled a glass with water and carried it toward her father's room. "I'll give Dad a drink. You can change in here."

He was grateful for the warmth as he changed hastily, piling on as much warm clothing as he could—jeans, shirt, sweater, two coats, and the old overalls on top of everything else. They almost fitted him now, filled out by the things underneath. She came back just as he finished struggling with the straps. Then he worked the blanket into a long roll and hung it around his neck like an enormous scarf.

"Ready?"

"Yes."

She picked up two boxes of matches and handed them to him. "Keep these in your pocket. The wind'll blow out the lamp a dozen times before you've finished."

"Thanks," he said wryly.

"Do you know the way?"

"I hope so."

"Go up past the drafting yards, across the pasture paddock for a mile or so, over the little humps, down into the dip by the water troughs, and up the slope the way we always go to the top of the headland."

"I think I can manage it."

"There's not much moonlight, so you'll have to watch your step."

"I'll try."

"Whatever you do, don't go too far to the right. There are loose stones on the slope there right down to the edge of the cliffs."

He picked up the carton and the lamp. "Wish me luck."

She came over and put her hand on his arm, looking at him intently with her seeing eye. "Be careful, Joe," she said earnestly. "Please be careful."

He felt buoyed up, warmed by her concern. "You bet."

"Don't stay too long."

"Just long enough for someone to get the message."

"I'll wait up for you. I'll go in and sit with Dad."

He lumbered out of the door into the night, where the darkness enveloped him as if he had suddenly walked into a vast black cave.

11

Joe now started out on his own personal Calvary. His heart quailed as he stumbled up past the sheep pens in the gloom, straining desperately to see even the most obvious things. Although his eyes adjusted slowly to the darkness, it was still impossible to walk with certainty. His feet struck unseen stones or clumps of grass or stepped unexpectedly into ruts and holes, so he constantly jolted his spine and kinked his neck.

Clutching the box and lamp, he developed a shambling, shuffling walk in self-protection. All around him the landscape of the night was strange and frightening. Nothing seemed familiar anymore. The daytime paddocks were seas of darkness, the hollows were black and edgeless gulfs, the knolls and headlands were vague humps against the faint starlight of the sky.

He wondered how he could possibly have thought the island was beautiful. It now seemed a savage place, aloof and malicious. Several times he was on the point of turning back, convincing himself that it was too dark, too threatening, too dangerous. But the fear that Meg would call him a coward, and the knowledge that her father was lying there in agony waiting to be rescued, drove him on. He finally negotiated the pasture paddock, stumbled through the dips and hummocks beyond it, and descended toward the hollow where the spring-fed water ran.

"Be careful down there," Meg had said. "Don't get bogged, and don't fall into the sunken troughs. It might be better if you crossed farther up."

But where was farther up? He was getting confused. The low-lying ground was darker than dark, and the starlight was too faint to guide him. He hoped there were no open wells or patches of quicksand near the springs, or he would most likely take his last step and disappear from the earth forever.

It was the Black Bluff itself that saved him from disaster. He saw its silhouette against the sky and recognized the long slope of the shoulder that he and Meg had climbed before. It gave him a sense of direction. He was able to veer upstream, cross the hollow safely, and move onto higher ground.

And so at last, straining and panting, he neared the top of the headland—a boy shrunk to a speck in that vast primordial landscape, crawling like a black mite up the side of the sky. As he reached the summit, the wind seized him, buffeting his body and clutching at his clothes. The sound of the sea seemed frighteningly near, crashing at his feet, but he knew that it was really far beneath him at the bottom of the hideous gulf of darkness nearby.

He put down the carton with the lamp in it and fumbled in his pocket for the matches. Then, crouching protectively on knees and elbows, he lifted up the cardboard flap and struck a light. It was blown out in an instant. Twice more he tried, and twice more it had gone before it had even flared. Panic swept him—a fear that despite the agony of his journey he would fail to send a signal after all.

He took the rolled-up blanket that was coiled around his neck, draped it over the carton like a tiny pup tent, and crawled under it with his head and shoulders. There, after a good deal of groping and fumbling, he was able to strike another match and hold the flame against the wick long enough for it to catch. Then he hastily lowered the glass chimney and imprisoned the flame in calm and safety. Success. Elation. He positioned the lamp carefully under the vent that Meg had cut in the cardboard and pointed the mouth of the box vaguely toward the wide strait that separated Wayward Island from the mainland. The Special Patent Blake Signaling Lamp was ready to begin.

Lying on his left elbow, he took the hinged lid in his right hand and raised and lowered it quickly three times to give three short flashes. Dot-dot-dot. He paused momentarily and then raised the lid more slowly three times to give three longer flashes. Dash-dash-dash. Another brief pause and finally three more short flashes. Dot-dot-dot. He had sent out one complete S.O.S.

After a few minutes he decided that he should be counting the number of distress signals he was sending. He began to do so aloud, mumbling to himself rhythmically: "Dot-dot-dot, dash-dash-dash, dot-dot-dot. One. Dot-dot-dot, dash-dash-dash, dot-dot-dot. Two . . ." When he had counted up to ten he paused to wrap the blanket around his shoulders more closely, shielding his ears and the back of his head from the icy bite of the wind. After another ten he changed the angle of the carton, arguing that its position would be critical to a moving boat because the crew would be in a direct line of sight with it for only a short while.

By the time he had counted to a hundred he was numb. His right arm was aching and his body was shriveled with cold. The wind seemed to have rubbed his cheeks as smooth as polished pebbles. He stood up, stretched his cramped limbs, and peered down at the lamp through the open vent. It was still burning brightly, but he had no idea how long the kerosene was going to last, especially as the tank had been less than half full to start with. The thought made him uneasy and strangely afraid.

He rubbed his hands and cheeks, blew on his fingers, and crouched down to begin another cycle. He calculated that if he allowed a pause of five or ten seconds after each complete S.O.S., he could send out four signals a minute, or twenty in five minutes. A hundred would take him almost half an hour.

As he worked he kept changing the direction in which the mouth of the carton pointed. It was like varying the aim of a gun. He tried to guess the position of Cockle Bay so that he could point toward it, but then he told himself not to be stupid. It would have needed a lighthouse beam of a million candlepower to reach the mainland. What could he expect of a stable lamp in a cardboard box?

As the cold ate into his bones, he found it harder and harder to keep going. He had to set himself shorter goals—at first twenty signals followed by a rest to rub himself warm, then ten, and finally only five. But he finished another cycle of a hundred at last and sat hunched in his blanket, crouching low like a wounded animal in a makeshift hide. His lacerated finger where he had torn the nail from the quick in his desperate struggle to open the life-raft locker was hurting terribly in the cold—a fierce pulsing pain like a hot skewer being driven regularly under the nail.

He began to feel the hopelessness of everything. What was the use? Who was ever likely to see a pitiful little wink of light in that endless wilderness of ocean? In a fit of anger he seized the box and pointed it toward the west, toward the void of the Great Bight, and sent off his message like a plaintive cry. S.O.S., it went. S.O.S., S.O.S., S.O.S. With a sob he turned it wildly to the south and flashed his plea toward the wastes of Antarctica, and then north again toward the Australian mainland.

In his mind's eye he began to have dreams of rescue, visions of great ships coming into sight, liners lit up in the night, all signaling back urgently to him. He couldn't read their Morse, but that was unimportant. The message was always clear: His distress signal had been seen and help was on the way.

But then the reality of his plight came back to him—the cold and the helplessness, the pain and loneliness. In his despair he couldn't even remember whether he was sending out the right message, whether perhaps it should have been three dashes first and three dots in the middle. A fierce gust of wind suddenly whipped over the crest of the bluff and almost overturned the carton, lamp and all. The flame fluttered madly as if in panic. Joe dragged his possessions back a few yards down the slope, to the shelter of a rock he had glimpsed in the beam of light. It was no bigger than a sheep, but it gave him some protection. Once there he lay down in the blanket with his arm around the carton, waiting and thinking.

He decided that he would have to stay for at least one more cycle of a hundred signals. Who could know how near or how far a rescue vessel might be? A container ship or a tanker could be coming from the west at this very moment, just over the horizon, with the crew vigilant and the lookout alert. A tuna clipper could be heading for home after its last trip for the season, or a fishing boat making for Cockle Bay with Stewy Sampson or Tiny Mazerakis at the helm. Any one of them might catch a glimpse of that winking light high on the top of Black Bluff and tingle with alarm at what it was saying, at its terrifying universal message: *Save Our Souls, Save Our Souls, Save Our Souls*. Joe knew that he had to try again. He would wait awhile and then try again.

He looked down at the lamp through the vent. It was idiotic to waste fuel while he was waiting. What would Meg think if the light failed just as a ship passed by? He reached inside, turned the wick back to a glimmer, and blew sharply down the glass chimney. The rind of blue light disappeared in an instant, and darkness enveloped him fearfully again.

He lay quite still, peering into nothing. The night was full of menace. The wind mourned in the rocks, the sea surged spitefully, the tussocks hissed and whipped the bony slopes below. There were other sounds too, strange unidentifiable sounds suggesting stealthy movements in the night. He looked around quickly, afraid that something or someone was creeping up behind him, but it was impossible to see anything an inch beyond his nose.

His scalp prickled at the thought of unknown things, evil things, on the Bluff beside him. Ghosts perhaps. Hadn't a sealer or whaler long ago gone over the cliff to his death, so Uncle Harry said? He had been pushed, murdered in this wild, lonely place, and was his ghost now wandering about vindictively forever on this hill? And the little girl who had died back at the cottage, and the sailors who had been drowned? Surely in a place like this their ghosts would wander endlessly looking for peace and rest.

After a while Joe couldn't bear it any longer. His nerves were raw. He hastily fumbled for the matches and lit the lamp again. As he held the flame to the wick, he could see his hand trembling. He took the carton and his blanket and went up onto the exposed knob of the Bluff once more. He felt insignificant. In all that infinity of sea and sky he was less than a dust mote. Even the island he was standing on was no more than the head of a pin. In such a vastness of space, how could human beings be so presumptuous about their importance? How could they think they mattered? And how could he and Meg and poor Uncle Harry hope to be rescued?

Yet human beings battled on. They refused to give in. They struggled and improvised. That was one of the most enduring things about them.

Joe wrapped the blanket around his frozen shoulders, knelt beside his ridiculous cardboard box, and began the agony all over again: S.O.S., S.O.S., S.O.S. His finger burned with pain, his arm ached, and his eyes watered in the wind. At times they were so bleary that he had to wipe them constantly with the ball of his hand, fearful that he wouldn't even see a ship if it passed right in front of his nose. Perhaps his eyes were not only wet from the wind but from tears of frustration too.

He wondered whether he would ever reach a count of a hundred this time. It was like climbing an impossible mountain, an Everest far beyond his reach. He struggled to twenty and then to thirty. It would have been so easy to give up at that point, to say he had done his best, and to blunder back to the cottage, to Meg, to the beckoning kitchen fire. The fire. The thought of its warmth almost tipped the balance. But then he remembered the responsibility that lay on his shoulders, his promise to Meg, his duty to Uncle Harry. He wrapped the blanket more tightly, steadied his chattering teeth, and went on doggedly once more. His count rose to forty, crept painfully to forty-five, and at last

reached fifty. It was a milestone that deserved rec-
ognition. He stood up in the buffeting wind, wiped
his eyes, rubbed his cheeks, and ran briskly on the
spot to stir up his circulation.

As he knelt down again to continue the cycle, he
wondered whether he shouldn't be angling his
message at the sky as well as the sea. There were
airways up there, flight paths for the big jet airliners
traveling between Adelaide and Perth that often
passed almost directly overhead. But he rejected
the idea. The lamp would slide backward and tilt
on its side, with the flame blackening and cracking
the glass chimney and the fuel draining away from
the wick. He would have to go on as he was.

Slowly the count crept up to sixty and then to
seventy and on to seventy-five. He was so numb
with cold that he was past thinking. The movements of his hand were as jerky and automatic as
the arms of a robot, his counting as mechanical as
a machine. But he kept on relentlessly, refusing to
let his body give up until the next goal had been
reached. And so he rose slowly up the mountain
of numbers he had to climb until he reached the
summit, the final century. Then he stood up and
peered all around at the cold and unresponsive
darkness for the last time before snuffing out the
lamp, picking up the blanket and box, and shambling off down the shoulder of Black Bluff toward
the cottage.

He knew he had failed, but he was past caring.

Nobody had answered his light, nobody had even seen it. He had tried, God knew how he had tried, but the world had ignored him. Perhaps he had expected too much in the first place. What was the use of a little lamp in the Antarctic Ocean? It was like lighting a match in outer space and asking someone on Earth to see it.

He fell twice on the way home, but luckily neither the lamp nor the mirror was broken. He lost his way after crossing the freshwater gully and veered too far to the right. He was within a few hundred yards of the south coast before he realized what had happened, and so he had to turn at right angles and head back across the island toward the opposite shore. Even then he didn't know where he was until a light shone out clearly ahead. Meg, bless her, had put the lighted candle in the window to guide him home. Joe lifted his leaden legs and quickened his step. He suddenly understood the old stories about lighted windows that guided the fishermen home from the sea and the hunters home from the hill.

She was waiting at the door when he stumbled in. She hadn't slept, hadn't even rested. Most of the time she had sat silently by her father's bedside, keeping him warm with extra blankets as he went more deeply into shock, moving quietly back and forth from the bedroom to the kitchen to stoke the fire or heat the water. She looked at Joe anxiously as he took off the blanket and put down the box.

"Any luck?"

He shook his head. "Didn't see a thing. No boats, nothing."

She lowered her gaze in disappointment. "It was worth a try."

"How's your dad?"

"Bad."

"I should have stayed up on Black Bluff, but I couldn't stand it any longer."

"You stayed long enough. I was getting worried about you. I didn't like the thought of you sitting up there by yourself on that cliff in the dark."

"I didn't like being there," he answered honestly.

"Better stay by the fire and thaw out. Would you like some hot tea?"

He almost drooled. "Anything warm, anything for my stomach. It's starving."

Her tone was rueful. "We'll be starving for a long time yet."

He stood by the fire, gratefully warming his body. As she bent to lift the hot water, the firelight caught her face and lit up the great bruise there—the contused blue-black flesh, the closed eye, the swelling.

"You look awful," he said. "You ought to be in bed."

"I wanted to wait for you."

He watched her as he sipped his drink. She was tough. Many a person in her position would have given up long ago. He remembered hearing once that women and girls were better at enduring pain, that they could cope with hardship, that they had some kind of inner strength. Well, maybe Meg was like that. She was proving it now.

While he drank she slipped into her father's room once more and returned as silently as she had gone. "He seems to be a bit easier," she said. "Or maybe he's in a coma." She paused. "You'd better go to bed. It's after midnight. Take the blanket."

"What about you?"

"I'll lie down here on the bunk by the fire."

He blundered into the door as he went out. "Can you find your way?" she called. "The bed's near the window."

"I'll strike a match," he answered.

A few minutes later they were both asleep. Outside, the huge sky arched impersonally above the little cottage where they lay, the wind moaned, the island crouched obsequiously in its endless ocean. They were locked in a prison of solitude and silence, and nobody in the whole world had any inkling of their fate.

12

When Joe woke up in the morning, Meg was already busy. She had stoked up the fire, heated some water, and washed herself. She had been outside gathering wood, checking her distress signal, and rummaging about in the shearing hut. And she had been in to see her father. He was conscious and spoke to her briefly, but he seemed vague and uncertain. The pain was still unbearable and his mouth was dry.

Joe walked into the kitchen shamefacedly. "I'm sorry," he said. "I just didn't wake up."

"I'll forgive you this time," she answered briskly.

He wondered whether her face was a little less bruised this morning, and her eye a little less swollen. Perhaps he was imagining an improvement in the light of day after watching her in the gloomy firelight the night before.

"I want you to stay here with Dad," she said, "in case he calls for something."

Joe was surprised. "Why? Where are you going?"

"To catch some breakfast."

He chortled. "Worms and grubs?"

"No, fish. Whiting."

His eyes opened wide. "Fish? Have you found a fishing line?"

She took a rusty cracker can from the table and held it up. "I remembered this during the night. Herc Sampson left it in the shearing hut years ago—some old hooks and sinkers, and a couple of lines. I'll try fishing from the landing; we often get whiting there."

"What about bait?"

"Cockles."

He looked at her in admiration. "Gee, you're a trouper, Meg."

She headed for the door. "I hope I won't be long."

He called after her. "Two'll do me, two *big* whiting. I'm so hungry I could eat a slice of Scarface."

It was painful for him even to think about food. He wondered how starving people felt, people lost in the wilderness, people marooned on a desert island. What was he saying? They *were* marooned on an island. He contemplated that idea for a minute but then dismissed it. They were not really trapped hopelessly without food. Apart from the fish that Meg was trying to catch, there were cockles in the sand, limpits and razorfish in the rockpools, young seabirds and eggs on the cliffs of the headlands. And there were sheep—he could see some of them through the open doorway grazing contentedly not far away. He doubted whether he could kill and skin one, but Meg could probably do it if she had to. She seemed to be able to do most things.

He heard a cough and a groan next door and hurried in to see what was the matter. He felt afraid and terribly helpless. Uncle Harry was lying back with his eyes open, fully conscious.

"Hello," Joe said, smiling feebly.

"That you, Meg?"

"No, it's Joe."

There was silence for a while. "Nice old mess," Uncle Harry said at last. His voice was something between a croak and a whisper. "Always preaching about gas. Especially at sea. And look what happens."

It was true. Joe knew that normally no one was more careful with gas than Uncle Harry—not only on his boat but in his service station too. And yet he had blown himself up. It took only one mistake, and he had made one.

"We'll have to get away from here, Meg," he said.

"Joe."

"Yes, Joe."

Joe tried to reassure him. "It won't be long, Uncle Harry. Someone is sure to come."

He looked carefully at his uncle's face and hands. They were not really too badly burned. There was none of that terrible gray ashy-looking flesh that someone had told him indicated a very deep burn. There were not even many red, moist-looking blistery patches that went with second-degree burns. And the total area was not large. Of course Uncle Harry looked monstrously ugly without his hair or eyebrows or eyelashes, and with his parched lips, but Joe hoped fervently that he wasn't going to die. He felt sure that he could be saved if only they could get him to the hospital—unless he had inhaled so many gasoline fumes that the fire had raced into his nostrils and exploded inside his throat and lungs, burning the lining and destroying the tissue. He hoped there hadn't been time for him to breathe in enough vapor for that to happen.

"No radio," Uncle Harry said suddenly.

"No."

"Not here in the cottage. Only on *Seahorse*."

"*Seahorse* is gone."

Uncle Harry sighed as if accustoming himself to a very painful thought. Although his concentration seemed to waver now and then, his memory was good. "Who got the raft out?"

"I did."

"From the locker?"

"Yes, before the whole boat went up."

"Just in time?"

"Yes, just in time."

His uncle seemed pleased. "Good work, Joe."

Joe looked at his torn fingernail. The finger still throbbed with pain. Clearly it was going to remind him of the incident for days to come.

There was a pause. "How long have we been here?" Uncle Harry asked.

"Since lunchtime yesterday."

It took a while for the information to sink in. "And now we have to wait for a boat?"

"Yes, for Stewy or Mick or someone."

Uncle Harry suddenly winced as if struck by a wave of pain even more shocking than the agony he was enduring all the time. He groaned and shivered. Joe moved forward in alarm. "Are you all right, Uncle? Can I get you a painkiller or something?"

Uncle Harry let out his breath slowly in a kind of whistle. "No . . . I'll be all right, Joe. Just leave me for a bit."

Joe walked out of the room on tiptoe. He didn't quite know why. He went outside and was about to run down to see if Meg had caught anything when he saw her racing up toward him. She was carrying three nice fish on a wire loop threaded through their jaws, but instead of using the usual path that led up from the landing, she was hurtling along an old track behind the house. He waved and called out excitedly, "You beauty."

She didn't smile or raise her catch boastfully but kept on running until she was within a few yards of him. He could see at once that something was wrong.

"Meg?" he said anxiously. "Meg, what's up?"

She stopped in front of him at last, panting hard. "Oh Joe."

A strange panic seized him. "Meg, for God's sake, what's up?" It was clear that something terrible had happened. "Meg, tell me."

"Oh Joe," she repeated, trying to get back her breath. "Joe, I've found Mophead."

Joe's heart skipped a beat. "Mophead?" he shouted. "Is he alive?"

She looked at him sadly and slowly shook her head. His hopes were crushed in an instant. "Tell me then."

"Come with me."

She turned and led the way back in the direction from which she had come. He followed her, torn in a dozen ways by dread of the horror he knew he had to face. As they came down the slope above the highwater mark, she veered off the path to the left. The ground was quite untrodden, dotted with occasional tussocks, bushes, and large patches of open sand.

Something was lying on one of the sandy patches. At first Joe thought it was a small heap of kelp or seaweed thrown up above the tidemark by the wind, but then he saw a long track like a turtle's trail leading up to it, as if something had been scrabbling and dragging itself slowly up the sandy slope. As they came nearer, he saw two legs protruding from the heap, and then a nose and two floppy ears. It was the body of a dog. It was Mophead.

With a cry Joe sprang forward and flung himself down beside it. He lifted the head from the sand, hoping desperately that the eyelids would blink, the eyes move, the dear old mouth spread into its special kind of grin. But the head lolled lifelessly in his hands. He put his fingers on the burned and charred coat, and held the seared paws silently. And then a great sob welled up from his chest and choked his throat.

"He's dead, Meg," he sobbed. For Joe, no greater word of grief could ever have been uttered.

She nodded. "He's only just died. His body is still warm."

Big teardrops were trembling on the lower lids of Joe's eyes.

"How . . . how did you find him?"

"I saw the marks on the sand. He must have got ashore somehow yesterday and tried to crawl up to the house."

Joe was devastated. "Oh God, he was probably here all night. If I'd known, I could have saved him."

She shook her head. "He would have died, Joe.

He was too badly burned. And he couldn't walk. I think his hip was broken."

Joe knelt over the body with his head almost touching Mophead's face. "Oh Mophead," he said. "Poor happy Mophead. And it was all my fault."

"No it wasn't."

"Yes it was. I should never have brought him on this trip."

He sat and looked up at Meg. Tears were streaming down his face, leaving shining trails on either side of his nose, wavering past his mouth, dripping off his chin. Meg sniffed and a tear ran down her face too. It came from her open eye, so her crying looked strangely one-sided. "We'll have to bury him, Joe."

"Dear old Mophead." Joe was gazing down at the crumpled body. "He was trying to reach us, Meg—to drag himself up there. He knew where we were. He tried and tried but he couldn't reach us."

"He was trying to reach *you*, Joe. He wanted to be with you right up to the end. You were the only real friend he ever had. He loved you, Joe."

Joe tried to say something but it stuck in his throat. A wave of sobbing shook his shoulders and he tried again. "He was my friend, Meg."

She nodded. "I know." She held out her hand. "Come. We'd better go."

He stood up slowly, wiping his eyes with the backs of his hands.

"We'll come back in a little while," she said gently. "First we'll find out how Dad is. I'll see if he can eat a bit of grilled fish." They turned and walked sadly up toward the house.

Later on that morning they went back to bury Mophead. Joe took a pick and a shovel and dug a grave in the small hummock overlooking the head of the cove. Then they carried the body up from the beach and laid it gently in the dry earth at the bottom of the hole. Joe started filling it in, but when the first shovelful of soil fell silently on what was left of Mophead's coat, Joe's tears blurred his eyes so much that he couldn't see what he was doing. Meg took the shovel from him quietly. "I'll finish it," she said. But Joe shook his head. "He'd want me to do it, Meg." She understood and handed back the shovel.

When the task was finished, they smoothed the sides of the mound and put up a post at the head of it. Then Joe took his knife and, in spite of the broken handle, managed to carve MOPHEAD on a piece of board and wire it onto the post at right angles. They both stood looking at it.

"One day I'm coming back with a proper notice on a piece of copper," Joe said. "Then it'll last for a hundred years."

They started to walk away. Halfway back to the cottage Joe turned and gazed back at the post standing against the skyline above the bay.

"I think Mophead would be happy there," he-said. "The land will always be open and free, with the bay below, and the sand and the sea that he always loved."

Meg pressed his arm. "I'm sure of it," she said.

Throughout the rest of the day there was no sign of help—no passing ship, no boat from the mainland, no airplane overhead. They enlarged and etched out their S.O.S. notices outside, ran up a bigger distress signal on the chimney pole, chopped more wood, and sat quietly beside Meg's father for long periods in the bedroom.

As he watched, Joe's mood varied greatly, swinging from despair to hope, confidence to fear. Sometimes Uncle Harry seemed strong enough to survive; sometimes Joe sat petrified, wondering what they would do if he died. Would they have to bury him like Mophead and put up a post to mark the spot? What would they tell Aunt Ellen when they were rescued—if they were ever rescued? The thought of everything they would have to face was too much for Joe. He stood up and quietly left the room.

There was no lunch, so they had to live on the memory of the fish they'd had for breakfast. Joe was eager to start fishing again, but Meg said the tide was out and so it would be a waste of time until later in the afternoon.

They sat in the kitchen for a while, polishing the lamp glass and the mirror again in preparation for the coming night. Meg said it was her turn to go up to the top of the Bluff, but Joe wouldn't hear of it. She bristled, thinking he was opposing it because she was a girl.

"No, no, it's not that," he said hastily.

"Why, then?"

"Because there's only an eggcup of kerosene left in the tank. You'd only just get up there and you'd have to turn around and come back home again."

She saw the point. "But we'll use up the bit that's left, won't we?"

"Sure, down here."

"From the top of the house?"

"No, from the high ground above the cove—the spot where we—" He stopped, unable to bring himself to say "where we buried Mophead."

"Where?"

"Where we were today."

She nodded. "Okay. I'll go up there as soon as it's dark." She hesitated and watched him closely for a minute. "Actually I'm glad I don't have to go up on Black Bluff. I would have been scared up there all alone." She paused. "Were you scared, Joe?"

He was about to tell a lie but then decided that it would be stupid. "I was scared stiff," he answered honestly.

"Maybe the hillock by the cove will do just as well."

He was despondent. "No, I'll bet it won't do any

good. We might as well be in the middle of the Pacific Ocean or the Sahara Desert for all the help we're likely to see."

"We might be lucky."

"Not likely. I'd like to know what all the boats from Cockle Bay are doing. They must be hugging the mainland. And what about Andy Jones? You'd think he'd be suspicious by now."

"Not before tomorrow night or Thursday."

"You'd think he'd want to know whether we've loaded the sheep or not."

She looked at him shrewdly with her peculiar one-eyed squint. "As a matter of fact I've been thinking about that. I think we should get them ready tomorrow—and the barge too, after breakfast at high tide."

He was confused. "What do you mean?"

"We could cull out the hundred ewes that have to be sold and pen them up. Then we could shift the barge from its mooring so that it's ready for loading. When a boat comes to rescue us, it can load the sheep straight away and take them back with us."

"But that's crazy. We can't do it on our own."

"Who's going to do it then? Dad?"

"Of course not."

"Well?"

"It'll just have to be left until another time."

"Another time will be too late. Dad needs the

three thousand dollars, remember? He needs it by Friday."

"But we don't even know which sheep to catch. We might take the wrong ones."

"We need young breeding ewes, a hundred of them. They're easy enough to pick out."

"I don't think I could."

She ridiculed him. "Don't you even know the difference between a ewe and a ram?"

He blushed. "Of course I do."

"Well then?"

"There are other kinds of sheep, aren't there?"

She laughed. "A wether is only a castrated ram, and we haven't got many of those. Anyway, I can do the choosing if you help me yard them up."

He nodded in confusion. "Sure."

Every now and then one of them went out and climbed up to a vantage point—the roof of the house or the shearing hut or the knoll above the cove. From there they peered out over the sea, shielding their eyes from the westering sun and scanning the haze to the horizon, inch by inch, for the slightest telltale sign—a hull, a mast, a momentary reflection. But there was nothing.

At four o'clock Meg took her father some warm tea. He had had a small piece of fish for breakfast, swallowing it without much pain, and he seemed to enjoy the tea. It was a good sign. He was also breathing fairly well, which suggested that his throat and bronchial passages were not severely swollen or damaged. But if there was cause for hope, there was also still cause for fear. He seemed very weak. What if an infection set in and started to spread rapidly while his body could offer little resistance? There would be nothing they could do then except watch him while he died.

They were ravenous by now. At four o'clock they both went down to the landing with Herc's rusty cracker can. The life raft still lay on the sandy beach above the tide mark where they had left it. Joe pointed. "If we can't get a bite from the landing, we can use the raft."

She smirked. "Who's going to row it? We could never keep it steady in one spot. And then you'd put a hook through it and we'd sink."

"Maybe it's not such a good idea after all."

"It's a terrible idea."

She ran off to get some bait. There was a cockle bed in the curve of the cove, where she stripped off her jacket and jeans and waded out, digging in the wet sand with her fingers while the water lapped perilously close to her chin. When she had thrown out a couple of dozen big cockles, she pranced back to the shore, rubbed furiously at the goose bumps on her arms and legs, and put on her clothes again.

Joe had replaced the hooks and traces on the two lines and increased the weight of the sinkers so that they could make a longer cast. Meg put down a double handful of cockles on the deck and emptied one of her pockets with a clatter.

"Your coat'll stink," Joe said without looking up.

"Yours does now," she answered bluntly.

They baited two hooks on each line and moved apart a little distance so as not to cause a tangle. "Aim for the clear little patches in the middle of the weed," Meg said. She pointed. "You're sure to get something there."

She was right. Within five minutes they had their first bite, and in half an hour they had landed seven nice whiting. "Bless Herc Sampson," Joe said triumphantly. "Bless him and his rusty can."

"We'll bake them in the coals," Meg said. "They're beautiful done that way."

"I'm hungry enough to eat them raw."

"Don't boast."

"I'd even eat cuttlefish and leatherjackets."

She laughed. "Stop whining and carry this batch up to the house."

He glanced at her as he picked up his load—her face bruised, jacket wet and sandy, eyebrows singed, hair dirty and disheveled. "You're a mess," he said. "You need your woolly cap to cover yourself up."

"Thanks very much."

"Your hair is like a bird's nest."

"My comb was burned in *Seahorse*, remember? Anyway, *you're* no film star. You need a bath."

He grinned. "I'm too hungry to argue. Come on, at least we've got plenty to eat."

For the first time since they had stumbled ashore on Wayward Island, a lifetime ago, his heart began to lift. Perhaps their luck was changing. Perhaps the sea that had tried so viciously to destroy them was beginning to call a truce. Perhaps it realized that their spirits were not so easily broken after all.

13

The baked fish were a great success but the distress signals failed again. Meg made two trips out to the knoll in the darkness after tea, and then she and Joe went out together at midnight for a last attempt before the kerosene ran out. But though they flashed out their S.O.S. more than a hundred times, there was no response from the gulf of darkness before them, no flicker of light to show that any other human being on the planet was interested in saving their souls.

As they groped their way back to the cottage, Joe looked up at the huge sky above them, winking with stars that were millions of miles away.

"I never dreamed a place could be so lonely," he said. "We might as well be on Mars."

"It wouldn't be very nice to be here on your own."

"I'd go crazy. I think I'd jump off the cliff."

"That's because you were born in a city."

"I reckon anyone would go crazy after a while. Anyone at all."

She was silent for a second or two. "Not an Outback person. Not a hermit or a prophet. They like lonely places."

"Well I'm not a hermit or a prophet, and I don't want to be one."

She suddenly changed the subject. "It's Wednesday now, do you realize that? The start of the third day."

He grunted. "It seems like a thousand years."

They reached the cottage and went quietly into the kitchen. Meg put the useless lamp in the corner so that they wouldn't fall over it in the gloom, while Joe stoked the fire to give a bit more light. Then she lit the candle and tiptoed into her father's room. She stood watching him for a long time, shielding the flame with her hand so that the light wouldn't fall on his face. He lay so still that for a terrible moment she wondered whether he had died, but then she saw that he was breathing. Asleep or unconscious, at least he was still alive.

She found it hard to watch him lying there. At the best of times it was a disturbing thing to see a grown-up person struck down, suddenly weak and helpless, but it was far worse when it was your own father. He had always been so strong and self-reliant, a leader in Cockle Bay and a great believer in independence. She had never known him to be any different. He had never been sick. Yet now he was weaker than a child. A single second on *Seahorse* had changed his life.

She returned silently to the kitchen and blew out the candle. It had already melted to almost half its length, and she knew that when it was gone there would be no way of lighting her father's room. Already Joe was complaining that finding his bunk was like blundering about in the black dungeon at Luna Park.

"Stop bellyaching," she said. "Go to bed and see that you're up early. It's your turn to catch the breakfast."

"I'm getting sick of fish," he answered. "I prefer bacon and eggs."

"Sure, sure."

"Or sausages and eggs."

"Would you like them on toast?"

"Or chops and eggs."

"Good. The chops are walking around in the paddock, and the eggs are halfway up the cliff at Black Bluff."

"Gee you're tough, Meg."

Joe groped his way into his room and crawled fully clothed under his blanket. A few minutes later

Meg bedded down again on her bunk by the kitchen fire.

And so another night passed while the three of them lay there like human flotsam in their prison. All around, the sea fretted and bickered against the island shore; above them the stars wheeled as impersonally as fate. In the far universe the business of earthly human beings was about as important as the antics of a dust mote on the wind.

Joe was up first on Wednesday morning, mainly because his body was cold and cramped. He stumbled out in the gray half-light, looking for the fishing can and the spare cockles they had put aside in a jar of seawater.

Meg stirred drowsily. "What time is it?"

He tousled her hair. "Fishing time."

She swung her legs over the side of the bed, stretched her arms, and yawned enormously. "Gosh I'm tired. I slept like a rock."

Suddenly she sprang up and ran across the room in her bare feet. "How's Dad?"

"I haven't been in to see."

They both sidled through the door and peered into the bedroom. Meg's father was awake, or at least his eyes were open in a strained, staring way. Meg went over and knelt at his bedside. "Hi, Dad," she said softly.

"Hello, love." It was still the same croaky voice.

Joe moved forward. "How are you, Uncle Harry?"

He moved his head slightly. "About as fit as a lame tortoise." There was no humor in his voice.

Meg watched him closely. "D'you think you could eat some breakfast? Joe's going down to catch some fresh fish."

He sighed in pain. "Can try."

"Right. But exercises first. We have to keep your circulation going." She looked up quickly. "You go, Joe. I'll stay here with Dad."

It was a perfect day—calm and clear, with the dawn trembling in the east. For a minute Joe was full of joy at the loveliness of it, at the magic of the morning. It was as if the world had just been newly created. But the sight of Uncle Harry's face in his mind's eye, the agony in the sound of his voice, the hopelessness of their isolation, and the fruitlessness of their signals soon overwhelmed his joy. And when he looked up at the knoll above the bay and saw the post there with its crude crosspiece— Mophead's grave—the day was gray with grief.

The fishing was a failure that matched his mood. No matter how far he cast or how often he changed his bait, there wasn't the faintest nibble on his line.

"Too calm, I s'pose," he muttered to himself.

He moved from place to place and jiggled the line impatiently, but after half an hour he had to admit that it was all a waste of time. He reeled in, threw away the bits of bait, and trudged back glumly to the cottage.

Meg met him at the door. "Any luck?" she asked.

"Nothing," he answered bitterly. "Not even a touch."

She looked better. The bruise on her cheek was less angry, and the swelling around her eye had gone down so much that she could peer out of it with a kind of leer.

She tried to sound cheerful. "Never mind. There are still a few pieces left over from yesterday. We'll have to ration them out—a little bit for breakfast and a bit for lunch."

Joe winced. "Cold?" he asked. "Cold fish?"

"What else?"

He wrinkled his lip in distaste. "If we ever get away from this place alive, I'm not going to eat another fish for a year."

"Count yourself lucky. Without Herc's old box we'd be eating seaweed and limpets."

"I don't like them either."

"Sheep dung, then."

He rolled his eyes in disgust as she started dividing the remnants of cold fish into tiny portions. Joe made the tea and then the two of them sat by the fire picking at the bits like a couple of cave dwellers. When they'd finished, Meg took two of the best pieces in to her father. She was away a long time.

"I'm worried about him, Joe," she said softly when she finally returned.

"Bad?" Joe asked.

"I think he's hurt inside."

She saw the expression on Joe's face. "I don't mean his throat or lungs, but his body."

"From a blow? From the explosion?"

"From hitting part of the boat when he went over the side. He could have broken ribs or something."

They were silent, gazing miserably at the fire. "And another thing," she said. "I had a look at his legs this morning—the burned parts—when I made the bed. They're worse, Joe."

He nodded. "They're burned worse than his face and hands. The gas must have got onto his socks. It would have taken a while for the flames to go out, even in the water."

She gazed at him intently. "We have to get help, Joe. We just have to get help. Gangrene or something terrible could be setting in."

"It's a long time since it happened."

"If we don't get help, he'll die. I know he will." There was a catch in her voice.

Joe had never felt more helpless. "It's too far to swim to the mainland," he said. "If it were only a mile or so we could give it a try."

"It's too far and too full of sharks. No one could swim twenty miles in these waters."

"We could try the raft, but it would take a long time, paddling."

She shook her head. "We'd need a running tide and a tail wind. Even then we might be carried off to the south, and then we'd be lost forever."

"Well, there's nothing else we can do."

She sniffed and wiped her nose. "I wondered about a beacon, Joe."

"A big bonfire? Tonight?"

"Yes, up on the knoll. There's driftwood along the shore, and we could take more of the posts."

"Good idea. A big bonfire would show up a long way."

"Farther than the lamp. Even with a mirror the lamp's too weak."

"We should have done it right away—on Monday night."

"Didn't think of it."

"Okay, we'll build it this afternoon and light it tonight."

She got up. "First we have to separate the sheep."

He'd forgotten about the sheep. It seemed such a crazy idea that he'd dismissed it from his mind.

"Are you serious?"

"Of course I'm serious. I spoke to Dad about it."

"What did he say?"

"He was a bit vague, but he said we should do it—especially when I mentioned the three thousand dollars."

"What was he vague about?"

"He started talking about other things, about *Seahorse* and the insurance. He said there'd probably be an inquiry."

"About the way she sank?"

"Yes. It upset him so much that I don't think we should mention it anymore."

"Yes, it would only make him worse."

"I'm scared, Joe, really scared about everything."

Joe made for the door. "Come on, let's round up the sheep. It'll take your mind off your—off other things."

He glanced at her face as they set off across the paddock.

"Does that bruise still hurt?"

"A bit."

"It was bad, wasn't it? A lot worse than you said."

She shrugged. "It's getting better now."

He was aware of her strength. Although she had been in great pain, she had never complained, hadn't even mentioned it.

"You're a tough turkey, Meg. I don't know how you put up with the pain."

"It's over now."

"You're just like your mother. She's as quiet as a lamb but as tough as old leather."

Meg looked back at the hut. "I don't hear Dad complaining either, and he's in a thousand times more pain than I am—every minute of the day and night. That's why we have to get him to the hospital somehow."

"It's this damned island. I never dreamed it could lock us up like this, just like a jail."

They plodded on until they neared the sheep. At first Joe thought they would simply try to separate a hundred from the rest out in the paddock, but Meg laughed and called him a jerk.

"You'd need a couple of good sheepdogs to do that, and even then you might have trouble."

"Why?"

"Because sheep hate being split up."

"What are we going to do then?"

"Drive them up to the yards, all of them together."

"But we only want a hundred."

"That's right. We'll cull out the ones we want and let the rest go."

"The ewes, the young ewes?"

"Sure. You can help me catch them."

"I could never tell which was which."

She eyed him wickedly. "It's easy. You just open their mouths and look at their teeth."

He was about to back away when he realized she was pulling his leg. "Sometimes I hate you," he said sourly.

As far as Joe was concerned nothing was easy, not even bringing the flock together. The sheep had rarely been handled, and so they were as fidgety as grasshoppers. Again and again as he raced this way and that to head off the leaders, Joe thought of Mophead—how quickly he would have done it and how much he would have enjoyed himself. Instead he was lying under the ground by the cove, silent and motionless forever.

It took much longer than they thought to round up the stragglers and yard the whole flock. Although it was almost midday before they had finished, Meg decided to go right on with the culling. Joe tried to help, but he was rather useless, so he became the tally clerk, telling her from time to time how many more were needed to fill the quota. They had brought the number up to seventy-five when Meg straightened up abruptly in the dust of the yard and looked upward and westward.

"Listen," she said. "Listen."

He cocked his head, but the sheep were milling about and bleating so loudly that it was hard to hear anything clearly.

"What is it?"

"I thought I heard a—" Before she had finished the sentence she suddenly leaped up and hurtled out of the sheep pen as if she'd been fired from a rocket.

"A helicopter," she yelled. "A helicopter. A helicopter."

She was racing forward up the slope behind the shearing hut, pointing and waving madly. "Here," she yelled frantically. "Here, here."

Joe sprinted after her. They were both running with their eyes fixed on a point in the sky, their legs dashing on blindly over tussocks and stones. They could see the helicopter far to the northwest, the sound of its rotors coming to them in a muffled flutter. It seemed to have come from somewhere out to sea and was passing diagonally across their line of sight toward Cockle Bay.

Meg raced on recklessly, her feet flying, her arms swinging every which way. Joe tore off his shirt, put it on a stick, and waved it frantically above his head. They reached the knoll out of breath and stood gazing as the helicopter continued remorselessly on its way, dwindling quickly into a dragonfly, a mosquito, a speck. For a while it wavered like a mote in the haze and then disappeared altogether.

Meg didn't move. For a long time she stood staring fixedly at the empty sky, her chest heaving, her heart fit to break. At last she turned and walked back disconsolately toward the sheep pens.

"They didn't see us," she said bitterly. "They didn't even see us."

14

They worked in silence now, except for the sound of
Joe's counting and the hiss of Meg's breath. It was
hot, dusty work, but they managed it in the end,
and turned the rest of the flock into the paddock.
Joe was the first to mention the helicopter again.

"It must have come from the oil rig," he said.
"There's no other explanation."

"Why?"

"Where else could it have come from—Antarctica? There's nothing else out there except the sea."

"A ship?"

"No, it's the rig all right. They're still exploring
for oil—test drilling."

"Why would it fly toward Cockle Bay?"

"I don't know. But it flew over there once before, remember. It could be picking someone up or getting something important."

Meg was moody. "It doesn't matter much, does it? They didn't see us, no matter what they were doing."

Back at the cottage they tried to wash some of the grime from their faces and hands. Meg looked at the S.O.S. sign on the grass near by and laughed cynically. "They say that the new satellites in space can spot a milk bottle or a pair of shoes on the earth quite clearly. In that case, you'd think they could see that sign."

Joe waved his hands about, trying to dry them in the sun. "Cheer up, Meg. There'll be someone fishing out in the passage today for sure. It's a perfect day."

In the kitchen he stoked the fire and heated the kettle while Meg went in to see her father. "Lunch coming up in a minute," he called. "Cold fish and condensed milk."

Meg was back almost at once. "Come quickly," she said. There was something in the tone of her voice that frightened Joe. He followed her hastily into the bedroom.

"For God's sake," Uncle Harry was saying, "back, back."

Joe stopped short and automatically looked from side to side for the danger that his uncle was warning them about.

"Back," he said again. "No, no. Don't, don't."

He seemed to be in a frenzy, rocking his head and jerking his arms about. It was only then that Joe noticed the unseeing stare in his eyes. Meg knelt at the bedside. "Dad," she said gently. "Dad, it's all right."

Her father's mind was far away. "Huh, huh," he said as if shocked by a sudden surprise, and then went off into a succession of moans and mumbles that made no sense at all.

Meg's face was white. "He's delirious, Joe. He doesn't know what he's saying."

Joe was as helpless as she was. He had never seen a delirious person before.

"It's the pain," Meg said. "The burns and the injuries inside. And not having any treatment at all."

"Shall we give him some more painkillers? Then maybe he'd go to sleep."

She was at her wits' end. "I don't know. I just don't know."

They looked at one another helplessly. "We have to get help," she said desperately. "If we don't get help today it'll be too late."

Joe hated inaction. He couldn't bear sitting about in times of crisis because it only increased his feeling of hopelessness. When things were bad, it was always best to be moving about, working, doing something. "I'll make the tea," he said, "and then I'll go out and build the beacon."

She looked up. "Where are you going to put it?"

"On Mophead's little hill, just as we said."

"Wouldn't Black Bluff be better?"

He shook his head. "We'd never be able to drag enough stuff up there for a decent bonfire."

"I guess not."

Soon after lunch Meg left her father, who seemed to have drifted into sleep, and joined Joe searching for driftwood. Every now and then they looked up and scanned the sea from horizon to horizon, but there was never a ship or boat in sight. They each carried up an armful of wood and heaped it in a crude pyramid on top of the knoll. Then they went over and started to tear off bits of timber from the shearing hut.

"We're like a couple of cannibals," Joe said as he wrenched away a loose board.

Meg was wrestling with a wooden strut. "Perhaps it's just as well poor Dad can't see us."

They were about to drag their loads across to the beacon when they both paused suddenly, dropped everything, and raced out into the open.

"It's coming back," Joe yelled. "The helicopter's coming back!"

It was true. They could see it now, a speck far out over the sea, flying diagonally across in front of them on the same path as before, but in the opposite direction.

Joe was beside himself. "It's on its way back to the rig. Come on, wave. Wave like mad."

He turned toward Meg, but she wasn't there. She was already out of earshot, hurtling down toward the cottage at breakneck speed. She plunged through the door, seized the carton that had served as their useless Aldis lamp, and wrenched out the mirror from the back. Then she came racing back up the hillock again, her feet scuffing bits of loose sand like a horse on a dune.

"Where is it, where is it?" she gasped as she arrived.

"There, there." Joe's finger trembled as he pointed.

"Oh yes, I see it."

Joe was mystified. "Are you going to shine that thing straight at them?"

"Anything to attract attention."

The helicopter was almost directly in front of them now, but still well beyond the island as it went puttering on its way. Meg held up the mirror to catch the sun and tilted it, trying to find the angle that would send a brilliant flash of sunlight toward the helicopter. It was like shooting a beam of light, a searchlight, at a target. When she judged the angle to be right she tilted the mirror quickly three times— flash, flash, flash.

Joe watched in astonishment. "Are you sending a message, an S.O.S.?"

"Trying to," she said, biting her lips. She sent three longer flashes and followed them with three short ones. "You do something too," she said without looking up. "Run around, take off your shirt, wave it in the air."

It was a bright afternoon with a clear sky and warm sunshine. There was no doubt that the mirror could send a shaft of light if only Meg could get it to shine at the pilot's eyes. But there was so little time to experiment. The helicopter was traveling quickly. Before long it would have moved so far toward the south that there would no longer be any hope of deflecting the sunlight toward it.

Meg moved the mirror feverishly, tilting it up and down, and from side to side, sometimes even dazzling herself as she leaned forward to try to judge where the reflection was going.

Their hearts began to sink. The helicopter continued to move on. It had reached its nearest point and was beginning to recede, shrinking second by second.

"Come on," yelled Joe. "Come on, look this way."

Meg was whispering a sort of prayer to herself. "Please. Please God, let them see it."

"That pilot must be blind," Joe raged. "Absolutely blind."

And then, just when it seemed certain that they had failed yet again, the helicopter suddenly turned sharply and headed toward them, descending as it came.

"He's seen us, he's seen us!" Meg shrieked.

Joe catapulted himself off the knoll, waving his

shirt above his head like a maniac. "Hey, hey," he shouted, "over here, over here"—even though the pilot had no hope of hearing him.

"Down to the house," Meg yelled. "He'll head for the house."

They tore down the slope past the sheep yards and rushed onto the open ground in front of the cottage. Meg held up the mirror and kept flashing out a constant stream of signals. The helicopter came toward them with astonishing speed. Within a minute or two it was crossing the coastline, and a few seconds later it rushed down on them like an angry bird, chattering furiously. Meg and Joe ran beneath it in a circle, looking up and waving. They could see the pilot and another man peering at them questioningly. Meg pointed to the S.O.S. sign, jabbing her finger forward at it as if to say, "Look, look, look." Whether the pilot actually saw the sign they didn't know, but the helicopter swept around them once more in a tight circle and started to land. It looked more than ever like a weird dragonfly—its bulbous head tilted down, its slender body tapering back, its rear rotor rearing angrily like a sting in its tail.

There was a turmoil of wind and flying flotsam, and the next moment it was rocking gently on the ground in front of them. The pilot and his passenger stepped out as Meg and Joe ran forward.

It was the same pilot who had warned the swimmers in Cockle Bay about Scarface. "Hi kids," he said breezily. "What's up?"

The story tumbled from them in disjointed bits. "It's Dad," Meg kept repeating. "We have to get him to the hospital. Right away."

They hurried inside. The pilot's passenger had taken an advanced course in first aid as part of his work on the oil rig, and though he was not a qualified doctor, he knew something about medicine. "Yes," he agreed as soon as he had looked at Meg's father. "He must go to the hospital. Immediately. He should have been there days ago."

The pilot ran back to his machine, and they overheard him talking urgently on the radio. "Yes," he was saying. "Yes, yes. To Ceduna Base Hospital. Yes. Burns from a gasoline explosion. Yes. Have I got the okay? Right. Yes, as soon as I can."

He came hurrying back. "I'll take your dad to Ceduna," he said to Meg. "Later on they'll have to decide whether to transfer him from there to Adelaide."

"We'll carry him on a mattress," the other man said. "I think we can just squeeze it in."

The pilot looked at Meg and Joe. "There won't be room for you two, though. Will you be okay on your own?"

Meg nodded. "Sure. But could you please call up Andy Jones in Cockle Bay if you can get through to him? We'll have to give him a message for Mom."

"No problem. I'll get through all right. I'll put out a mayday emergency call."

"No, don't do that," she answered quickly. "It'll frighten the wits out of Mom."

"Oh, sure. Tell you what. I'll get him on the intercom and hand over to you. You tell him what you want. And while you're at it I'll get things ready for your father."

They made contact with Andy a minute or two later. Meg started to tell him the whole story, but Andy suddenly interrupted her. "Your mom has just walked in," he said. "She was getting a bit worried because she hadn't heard from you. Why don't you speak to her yourself. I'll hand you over."

And so Meg found herself stammering out the story to her mother, trying not to alarm her too much. Her mother was shocked but calm. "Tell me, Meg, is he badly hurt? Tell me the truth."

Meg was in an agony, caught between doubt and hope. "He's burned on the face," she answered, "and on the hands and legs."

"Badly?"

"Well, pretty bad, I s'pose."

"Will . . . will he be all right?"

Meg had to fight to hide the quaver in her voice. "I . . . I hope he'll be all right."

"You only hope?" She could feel her mother's fear through the headphones.

"I don't know, Mom. Honest. When they get him

to the hospital, maybe everything will be a lot better."

There was silence at the other end for a moment. "I'll drive up to Ceduna right away," her mother said. "I'll try to get up there as soon as I can after the helicopter lands. I'll see you and Joe then."

"Wait, that's another thing." Meg didn't quite know how to break the news to her mother. "There's no room on the helicopter, so Joe and I have to wait here."

"*What?* All alone?"

"We've really been alone ever since the accident. We'll be okay." She was about to add, "But we're starving, and I've got a black eye," when her mother interrupted her. "I'll arrange for someone to pick you up—Mr. Sampson or someone."

"That's great, Mom. Could you tell him that he'll have to tow the barge back with the sheep? We've got them all penned up and ready. If Herbie Driver meets us with his truck and pays for them right away, we can still give Mr. Harding his money by Friday."

She thought she heard a catch in her mother's voice. "There's no need, Meg. It has already been paid."

Meg didn't understand. "What?"

Her mother hesitated again but then went on. "Mr. Lane has advanced the money. He insisted. He said that you three had saved his life. It was a debt he wanted to repay."

Now it was Meg's turn to stutter in astonishment. "But . . . but . . ."

"So there's no need to worry about the sheep. We'll discuss it all later. For the time being turn them out into the paddock again."

After all the trouble she and Joe had been through, Meg was tempted to complain, but she thought better of it. "Yes, Mom," she answered.

"I'll be in touch as soon as I can."

"Yes, Mom."

"Look after yourselves."

"Yes, Mom."

"Good-bye, dear."

"Good-bye, Mom."

As she finished speaking, the two men and Joe were already carrying her father out to the helicopter on a mattress. In the bright light of day he looked pitifully frail, nothing like the strong man who had been skippering *Seahorse* a few days earlier. His face was meaty red but there were few blisters. She took that to be a hopeful sign, even though he looked frightful. His lashless eyes and the singed remnants of his hair and eyebrows made him seem like the leader of some strange fanatical sect. His eyes were closed against the sudden sharpness of the sun.

There was some difficulty in getting him into the helicopter. They finally had to bend the mattress at right angles and jostle it aboard like a lounge chair. He groaned intermittently. Meg bent over him and kissed his forehead lightly. "You'll be all right now, Dad," she said. "You'll be in the hospital in less than an hour."

He made a sound, but she didn't know whether it was an answer or not. She didn't even know whether he was fully conscious or in a kind of coma.

The pilot and his passenger climbed aboard, the canopy snapped shut, and Meg and Joe stood clear. The main rotor turned faster and faster as the engine caught, and a moment later the helicopter rose, turned, and headed off across the sea toward the mainland.

After days of waiting in agony, the end had come with surprising suddenness. The whole rescue, from the instant when the pilot had first seen the flash of Meg's mirror to the present moment when his machine was disappearing into the distance on its way to the hospital, had lasted less than ten minutes.

They stood watching silently while the speck wavered and dwindled from sight.

"Well, that's that," Meg said at last.

"Didn't last long, did it?"

They were both suddenly at loose ends, thrown into a vacuum after the tension of the past few days. Meg put it into words. "I feel sort of empty," she said.

"I'm empty too," Joe agreed. "I'm starving."

She eyed him mockingly. "You know what I mean."

He laughed. "Sure. But my stomach's empty too."

She led the way back to the cottage. "What would you rather do then—clean up in here or catch fish to fill your stomach? Take your pick."

Even fishing had lost its attraction for Joe. "I'll flip you for it," he suggested.

They compromised by doing everything together. First they stripped the bunks, washed the bedding, and put the spare blankets back into the cupboards. Then they cleaned the kitchen, swept the floor, doused the fire, and buried the coals and ashes in the pit outside.

"The place looks cleaner than it has for ages," Joe said admiringly.

"It won't stay like that for long," Meg answered. "Not if Herc and Boxhead come over again. They're like a couple of pigs in a pen."

She heard the sound of bleating coming from the drafting yards and suddenly remembered. "Oh my gosh," she said, "the ewes. Come on, we have to let them out."

"Let them out? After all the hassle we had bringing them in and sorting them?"

"Don't argue. Come on."

It wasn't until he heard the details of Meg's radio talk with her mother that Joe felt better about it. "Good old George Lane," he said. "He's a champion, even if he didn't catch Scarface."

"He's a very kind man."

"He can afford it, though."

"That's not the point. He did it for us."

"He must have gone back to Cockle Bay after he had his arm stitched up."

"Well of course he did. He had to pick up his plane."

"I wonder if he'll ever come back to try to catch Scarface."

She shook her head. "Never. And Scarface won't come back either. He's too shrewd for that. He's been hooked twice; there'll never be a third time."

"Perhaps it's just as well. It's proper for him to be free, I reckon."

"So do I."

They took the fishing tackle down to the landing and cast out into their favorite spots—but without any luck. "Not even a nibble or a nudge," Joe said after half an hour. "Even the fish have gone away."

"Tide's out," Meg said.

"Tides, winds, clouds," Joe grumbled. "There's always something."

They sat in the sun for a while, idly flicking their lines.

"If Stewy doesn't pick us up today," Joe said, "I'm going to die of starvation. I couldn't spend another night on this hopeless island without something decent to eat."

"He'll come."

"Yes, but when?"

"About sunset. It'll take him three hours, at least."

They finally packed up and climbed the knoll behind the house to scan the sea for signs of their rescuers. Toward evening Joe gave a great shout. "Here they come."

It was *Petrel*, sure enough, charging down on Wayward Island at full speed. Meg ran back to the cottage, locked the door, and hid the key in its usual place under a loose brick. Then she and Joe went down to the landing to wait for Stewy and Boxhead.

It was a wonderful reunion. Mrs. Sampson had foreseen that Meg and Joe would be as hungry as sharks and had sent over a huge hamper of steak sandwiches, pies, pieces of chicken, sliced ham, buttered rolls, and thick slabs of fruit cake. And while they gorged themselves, Stewy brought up mugs of hot coffee from the galley and Boxhead gaped in astonishment at their story. Then they took the life raft on board, tied the barge to its mooring in Cay Cove, and headed for home in the gathering darkness.

They sailed into Cockle Bay shortly before ten o'clock, with the sea surging lazily against the headlands and the lights winking from the town. Joe stood on the deck watching. He felt as if he had grown three years in three days. An unbelievable experience was ending, an experience that had taught him much about the twists of fate, about other people, about himself. He had set out on a simple trip but had encountered disasters that had led to the death of Mophead, and almost to the deaths of George Lane and Uncle Harry.

Poor Mophead. He had set out so joyfully from this very spot only a few days earlier. Joe's heart ached at the thought.

And Scarface was free. He always would be. He belonged to legend now, the legend of Cockle Bay, just as Joe and Meg belonged to the legend of Wayward Island. Their story would live on for years to come.

For two or three days they stayed with Stewy and Mrs. Sampson until Meg's mother returned from Ceduna. Meg ran out to meet her. "How's Dad?" she asked breathlessly.

Her mother beamed. "He's going to be all right. They say he'll make a complete recovery."

Good luck seemed to be running their way at last. Not long afterward the insurance money was approved for the replacement of *Seahorse*, and a week after that Uncle Harry was discharged and sent home to convalesce. The burns, although hideously painful, had not been as bad as Meg and Joe had feared. Although he had suffered badly from shock, and was still nursing a cracked rib and bruised kidneys, his strength was returning quickly.

Meg's face was almost normal too. Her singed hair was growing again, and there was no sign of the bruise on her cheek.

Two weeks later Joe and Meg had their thirteenth

birthday. They exchanged presents before breakfast—a new pocketknife for Joe, a woolly cap with a pompom for Meg. Joe fingered the knife gratefully. "Thanks, sis," he said.

She eyed him whimsically. "I'm not your sister."

"Well, you seem like one now—a sort of sister and a pal."

All her brightness had returned. "I don't go much for brothers, but if I have to have one, I guess you'll do."

Her father walked in at that moment, stretching himself to test his strength.

"Herbie Driver is pestering me about those sheep," he said. "I don't suppose you two would like to lend a hand next weekend—over on Wayward Island?"